M298ℓ

the
last wolf
of
Ireland

ELONA MALTERRE

the Last wolf of Ireland

❀ ❀ ❀

CLARION BOOKS • NEW YORK

Author's note: Pronunciation of Gaelic may vary from district to district. For facility of reading, these Gaelic words may be pronounced in the following manner:

Breaghmhagh   BREEog-mog
Cuchulain   koo-HULL-in
dullahan   DOO-la-honn
Sdhoirm   sdorm

Clarion Books
a Houghton Mifflin Company imprint
215 Park Avenue South, New York, NY 10003
Text copyright © 1990 by Elona Malterre

Library of Congress Cataloging-in-Publication Data
Malterre, Elona.
    The last wolf of Ireland / by Elona Malterre.
        p.   cm.
    Summary: Despite the frightening stories they've heard about
wolves, a boy and girl, living in Ireland in the 1780's, attempt to
defy authority and save the last wolf left in the country.
    ISBN 0-395-54381-9
    [1. Wolves — Fiction.   2. Ireland — Fiction.]   I. Title.
PZ7.M29845Las   1990
[Fic] — dc20   90-30074
                                                   CIP
                                                   AC

BP   10 9 8 7 6 5 4 3 2 1

For my daughter Alexandra
and her friends,
Christine, Cathy, Joanna,
and for my nephews
and nieces.
And for Susan Scott,
who always believed
in this story.

❦

Acknowledgments

I'd like to thank my agent, Sherry Robb,
who loved this book. A special thanks
to Dorothy Briley and the fine editorial staff at
Clarion, whose care and skill
in editing are every author's dream.

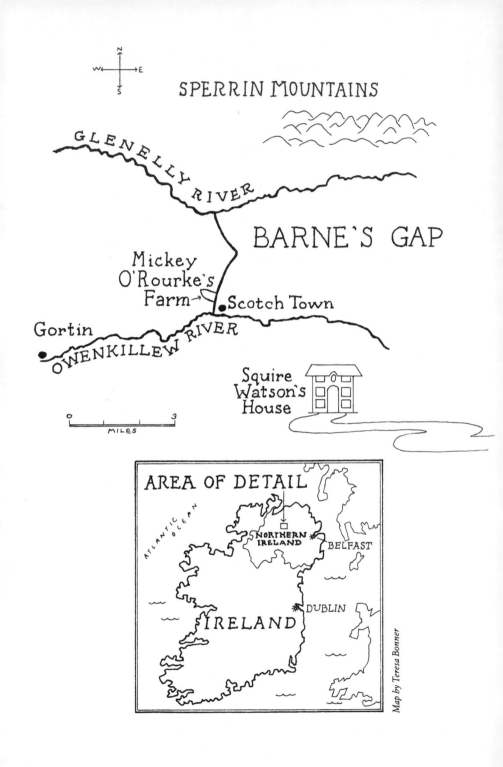

SPERRIN MOUNTAINS

GLENELLY RIVER

BARNE'S GAP

Mickey O'Rourke's Farm →

Scotch Town

Gortin

OWENKILLEW RIVER

Squire Watson's House

0 — MILES — 3

AREA OF DETAIL

ATLANTIC OCEAN

NORTHERN IRELAND

BELFAST

DUBLIN

IRELAND

Map by Teresa Bonner

The last wolf in Ireland was killed in a place called Barne's Gap in 1786. This is the story of that wolf, and of a boy and girl who tried to save him.

❧ 1 ❧

Devin O'Hara walked in the place once called Breaghmhagh, the Plain of the Wolves. But it was now named Barne's Gap, after an Englishman who drew maps. Devin had never seen a wolf here, although a long time ago at night he had heard one howling. It was a frightening, lonely sound. Devin's grandfather had told him that wolves stole sheep and cattle, and ate children and even men. His grandfather knew a man in the village who was eaten alive by wolves.

Barne's Gap had also been the place of robbers and highwaymen. Devin's grandfather would sit in front of the fire and tell stories. "Highwaymen with daggers this long," he'd say, and his eyes would bulge out. "They'd cut your head off if you sneezed. And the dullahans! They still travel there. Ghosts what travels in coaches, carrying their heads under their arms. Seen 'em meself."

"Now, Papli," Devin's mother would say. "Stop frightening the child."

"I'm not afraid," Devin would insist. Devin hated when his mother called him "child." The thought of it made him angry, and now, as he continued along Barne's Gap, he grabbed a stick and pretended to stab a ghost in the stomach and club another over the head.

Devin had blue eyes. His hair, the color of chestnuts that grew in trees along the roadside, kept falling in his eyes, but his mother only cut it at every second new moon. Cutting hair at any other time would bring ill luck.

Devin loved Barne's Gap. He loved the Sperrin Mountains rising to the north and the stone fences bordering the small fields. He especially loved the forest beyond, where he could clamber down one ravine and up another. And when the mist drifted down from the mountains, Devin grew frightened and excited at the same time. When the mist came, Barne's Gap was a different world, magical and mysterious.

The cornerstones of the fences stood like enemy chieftains, and Devin pretended to be Cuchulain, the best swordsman that ancient Ireland had ever known. Cuchulain had lived long, long ago. He could fight a hundred men at once and not suffer a single wound.

Devin stabbed at the air, at a cornerstone, and imagined what people would say: *There goes Devin, the bravest, strongest fighter in all of Ireland.* Even Paul Chandler, who bullied him because Devin was smaller, would say it.

As Devin played and walked, a mist was gathering in the distant mountains. The dullahans always came in a mist. But Devin wasn't afraid of dullahans. If he saw one, he would club it over the head. But then Devin remembered that dullahans didn't have heads. He grasped his stick a little tighter in his hand, and he began to wonder whether or not he should return home. Cuchulain would never return home. Cuchulain wouldn't be afraid.

The mist rolled like a great, gray beast, burying a distant hilltop; a blackthorn tree disappeared. Devin's grandfather had told him that sometimes the horses that pulled the dullahan coaches were headless too. The mist came closer. The forest to Devin's left had disappeared.

"An Irish mist is like no other mist in the world," Devin's grandfather always said. "Conjured up by the fairies to be hiding their mischief-making. And when the fairies is stirring and conjuring their mists, all manner of ghosts will be walking on this here earth, all rising from the bottom of lakes and graves. And they'll be walking on this here earth, looking for people to take away with them. Young and old they take. Especially boys."

The mist crept, then billowed, and suddenly Devin himself was caught up in the thick, gray fog. It was impossible for him to see either ahead of him or behind him. He pulled his sweater higher about his neck and turned for home.

But now, in the distance, he heard the rolling wheels of a coach coming. He could hear the clatter of stones, the driver racing. Only one man drove a carriage that fast — Squire Watson, the Englishman, the man who owned the big house south of Scotch Town.

There was a sharp bend in the road. The clatter came closer, faster and faster. Normal horses wouldn't be able to see the turn. It had to be a dullahan coach that was coming.

Devin ran toward the road edge where the forest grew. There he would be safe. The mist was thick. He could barely see in front of him. It was as though the forest had disappeared, had been swallowed by the great mist. Devin ran, but the forest was not where it should have been.

He felt as though he were running in a dream, as though his feet were made of huge stones, so heavy to lift, one after another; the coach was coming closer, and the mist seemed to hold his feet as though it were a great pot of glue that didn't want to let him go. The coach raced closer, and now he felt as though the wheels clattering across the stone were nearly on him.

Finally he reached the woods. Branches slapped at his face, tore at his clothes, but he didn't stop running. Broken twigs and branches lay on the forest floor. Devin tripped and fell headlong down a sharp bank, rolling and rolling senselessly through the thick, gray mist. Head over heels, toppling and turning, so that sky and ground were upside down and he didn't know whether he was falling from the sky or to the sky.

Devin was dizzy when he looked around. All he could see was the white-gray mist turning and boiling about him. The mist was so thick, down here where he was, that when he reached his arm out, he couldn't see the tips of his fingers.

He pulled his knees up under his chin and sat. Listening, he breathed as quietly as he could. There was nothing but silence. He always carried a rabbit's foot in his pocket for good luck, and he touched it noiselessly now. Still nothing but quiet. To his relief, the coach was gone.

But then from somewhere an owl hooted. He heard the breaking of branches.

He heard the sound again.

Devin leaped up. A tree branch cracked against his skull. For a moment, he saw a flash of brightness. Just as Devin fell again, he came face to face with a great black animal. It had a huge black snout and two yellow eyes burning through the mist, eyes the color of cat's eyes, but huge, the size of the sour green apples that grew along the roadside. Though he'd never seen one, Devin knew he faced a wolf.

He was immobilized with terror. He stared at the yellow eyes and they stared at him, holding him in a steady, unwavering gaze. If Devin had reached out with his fingers, he could have touched the wolf. He could smell the wild, damp fur smell.

Devin tried to speak, tried to shout. He knew that his mouth was open, but no words formed. The wolf stared back at him, the eyes like two small suns burning through the fog. Devin thought of his rabbit's foot, but he was afraid to move, afraid to touch it. The wolf snarled and he saw the white fangs. And then, without warning, it turned and disappeared in the mist, leaving Devin alone.

❀ 2 ❀

*t*here was no way for Devin to know that
the wolf he had seen was a female.

She had three pups hidden in a den nearby. Now,
anxious for their safety because the boy had been close
to the lair, she returned to her offspring.

The young wolves' keen sense of smell alerted them
that their mother was near even before they had seen
her, and they began to whine and wriggle their small
bodies with excitement. When she entered the den,
the cubs leaped at her with a joyful flurry of face licks.
She returned their eager greeting, wagging her tail and
whining, as her quick, pink tongue lavished affection
on their mouths, ears, and muzzles.

At three weeks of age, their eyes had not yet turned
amber but were a beautiful, clear blue. Their ears appeared too large for their heads and flopped forward,

making their faces look curious and mischievous. Their waking hours were spent in nonstop frolic, in tumbling and biting and play growls that stopped only when they flopped down and fell asleep or when they ate.

The cubs had just begun eating meat and already had sharp, pinlike teeth. In another two weeks they would be completely weaned. If the mother had managed to kill something, she would have fed the cubs the raw meat, but her hunt had been interrupted by the dangerous presence of the boy and she had nothing to offer them except milk.

Even as they suckled, the wolflings whined with hunger. The she-wolf would have to go out in search of food again.

Under normal circumstances the wolflings would not have been left unguarded, nor would the female have had to hunt alone. She would have been part of a pack, and one member would have stayed with the cubs, caring for them. The others would have gone out in a group, in search of large prey — deer or wild boar.

Contrary to what the village people believed, the pack did not regularly kill sheep, nor had it ever killed people. Like all wolf packs, it was extremely territorial and generally hunted only in its own terrain, the boundaries of which were clearly marked with urine.

Occasionally the wolves would kill a stray sheep, but ordinarily the pack didn't hunt domestic animals because they were guarded by dogs. Unless the wolves were extremely hungry, they preferred to lose a meal rather than trespass into what they scented as another canine's territory.

But things in the woods had changed. These days, the female wolf rarely heard the howling of other packs. Even the distant mountains, which once had echoed with the howls of many wolves, were now silent. Without understanding exactly what was going on, the she-wolf instinctively sensed that the forest had become a place of danger.

One by one, the members of her pack had disappeared. Seven wolves would go off hunting at dusk for a deer or wild boar, but only six would return. Six would go hunting, but only five would return. At night the remaining wolves in the pack lifted their voices to the moon, calling to their lost members, but their eerie, disturbing howls echoed across the hills unanswered.

The baying of domestic dogs came farther and farther into the forest, and more and more often she heard loud, frightening exploding noises.

When she whelped her current litter, only she and her mate remained of the former pack. Her mate was devoted to her, and each day he would bring her food to the entrance of the den. Because he by himself could not bring down larger prey, such as a deer, he brought rabbits and badgers and rats, and even fish.

The female would eat and return immediately to her small, mewing pups, licking them and nuzzling them and curling her body around them so they stayed warm when they slept.

But one evening he left to go hunting and didn't come back. She waited patiently for him to return. At each sound from outside her den, she perked her ears and listened, and if the sound was strange, she would lay her head over her pups, keeping them quiet, so as not to alert an intruder. If a hapless mouse or rat wandered into the den, she killed it and ate it. But small rodents were not enough food for a mother wolf, and finally hunger drove her from her den.

When she caught the scent of her mate, she loped more quickly along his trail. She found him in a shallow ravine.

She batted his paws with her paw and bit at them gently, attempting to get him to stand. But he did not move. The sulphur smell of gunpowder came from a hole in his chest. His ears and tail had been cut off. Whimpering, she nuzzled his wounds, then desperately licked them, attempting to heal them with her tongue. She knew he was beyond healing; her keen sense of smell had already told her he was dead, but she continued her attentions desperately, whining all the time. Finally she gave up. She sat on her haunches and lifted her head to the stars and howled hauntingly and mournfully for him, a primordial, dismal lament that the wind carried through the spruce and pine and into the mountains beyond.

Since the death of her mate, she'd been hunting by herself. Now the persistent wolfling whines told her that her pups needed more food. Preparing to leave, she stood and growled at her cubs as warning not to follow her.

She scurried out of the den, leaving the cubs alone once again.

3

Barne's Gap was bordered to the north by the Glenelly River, to the south by the Owenkillew River. Devin lived in a small town called Scotch Town on the banks of the Owenkillew.

A hard dirt road served as the single street in Scotch Town. On the north side of the town, the houses were built in the English style, two-story houses with wood trim and flagstone and tile roofs. On the south side, many of the houses were still built with thatched roofs. Large, round stones, tied with ropes and thrown over the thatch, kept it from blowing away during storms. The windows under the straw resembled eyes below shaggy eyebrows.

Chickens in the street picked busily at some grains of oats that had spilled from a passing cart. The hens scattered in wild fright, squawking and flapping their wings, as Devin ran through them.

Ahead, he saw Katey Sullivan. Her skirts swung back and forth as she walked, and her dog, Bebo, padded along beside her.

"Have you seen Jimmy?" Devin shouted. Jimmy and Devin had been best friends as long as Devin could remember, until Jimmy had started playing with Paul Chandler. Now when Devin told Jimmy about the wolf, Jimmy would be his friend again.

He didn't even given Katey a chance to answer. "I saw a wolf!" he yelled as he ran up.

"A what?" Katey had a roundish face with blond, curly hair that was always braided into pigtails. Today she wore green ribbons in her hair, a green skirt, and a green sweater. She had blue eyes and was almost half a head taller than Devin.

When Katey's dog heard Devin, she began to bark excitedly and wag her tail. Bebo was a taffy-colored collie with one blue eye and one brown eye. She was named after the Queen of the Fairies. Bebo jumped up at his chest, tried to lick his face, and barked loudly.

"Hush, Bebo," Devin said to her. "No sticks now. I saw . . ." But then Devin saw Jimmy O'Brien walking with two other boys farther down the street.

"Hey, Jimmy!" Devin shouted, and ran off. But when he came closer and saw who Jimmy was walking with, he suddenly slowed down. Jimmy was walking with Paul Chandler and Sean Campbell. Paul always teased Devin, called him shrimp. Whenever Paul got a chance, he would beat Devin.

But the excitement of what he'd seen made Devin forget his fear. He caught up with them and gasped, "I've seen a wolf." Devin held his hands out in front of him, trying to show the others how big the wolf had been. "A big wolf!"

"A wolf!" Jimmy's eyes grew enormous. He was a redheaded boy with so many freckles on his face, it looked as though he had sneezed into a bowl of bran. "Where?"

But Paul Chandler sneered. "You're a liar." Paul was a big bully, with hair the yellow-gray color of congealed grease and large, rough-knuckled hands.

"I'm not lying. I saw it, I tell you."

"It was probably that stupid dog of that stupid Katey," said Paul.

"It was a wolf."

"Then why didn't he eat you? A little worm the likes of you," and Paul shoved Devin.

Jimmy came between them. "Leave him be, Paul," he said.

But Devin stepped out from behind Jimmy. "Well, at least my name doesn't mean worm, like yours does."

In Ireland a family name often described the color of an ancestor's hair, where he lived, or what he did for a living. One of Paul Chandler's ancestors must have been a fisherman, for the name Chandler meant "worm" in the Gaelic of certain areas of the country, and referred to fishermen who used worms when they went fishing.

Paul struck out with his fist. Devin felt the rip of knuckles in his face before he fell.

"You're nothing but a lying runt! A shrimp!" Paul yelled at Devin.

"I'm not lying!"

"Liar! Admit it. Or I'll hit you again." Paul bent above Devin, fists ready.

"I did see a wolf!" Devin grabbed Paul's ankles, pulling him to the ground. He crawled up on Paul's chest. But Paul was much stronger and threw Devin off easily. Paul, on top, pounded his fists on Devin's face.

A crowd gathered. Men smoking pipes came out of the houses, and women, some wiping their hands on their aprons, some with their knitting needles and wool still in hand, came to watch too. So did children.

"Knock him with a chin-chopper, lad!" someone shouted eagerly. A fight, whether it was between two dogs, two cocks, two men, or two boys, was always watched with pleasure. Most of the bystanders cheered for Devin; Paul was not well liked. If Paul saw a dog or cat anywhere, he couldn't walk by without sending it a kick. Also, Paul was the butcher's son, and the butcher was always suspected of charging too much for his meat. The women claimed that Paul's father weighed the scale down, holding it with his big, hairy thumbs.

But some of the crowd cheered for Paul. Because he was winning, they had already begun to place bets in his favor.

Devin managed to throw up his hips and toss Paul off, as an unruly horse might topple its rider. He crawled to his feet. Blinded by tears and smeared blood, he grabbed in a confused, useless fashion at Paul's clothes.

This time, Paul threw a tremendous punch into Devin's stomach. Devin crumpled, gasping for air and clutching at his belly, feeling as though he would never breathe again. For a moment, everything went black. He felt the sour taste of his stomach rise to the back of his throat. But he would not be sick, he told himself. He would not let himself be sick. He tried to open his eyes. The crowd whirled around, some smiling faces, some jeering faces, but all were looking at him, and then Devin's eyes closed from the sick feeling in his stomach, and he started to cry.

❀4❀

Somehow, without opening his eyes, Devin knew that Paul was going to kick him in the stomach. Paul towered over him; Devin could feel him. He opened his eyes for a brief moment and saw the heavy leather soles of Paul's boots.

"Say you're a liar," Paul said. "Say you're a dirty, lying, wormy shrimp, or I'll kick your guts out." The brown, scuffed, heavy-soled shoes nudged Devin's chin. "Say it! Or I'll — "

"All right! 'Tis enough of your bullying."

Devin could hear the shifting of the crowd as it turned to face the speaker. Devin didn't recognize the voice. He saw the blurry outline of a broad, burly man.

Like the other men gathered there, and like Devin himself, the stranger wore rough woolen knee breeches and woolen knee socks. The man wore a gray woolen sweater under a leather vest. He carried a traveling bag in one hand and a silver-handled walking cane in the other.

"You won't be kicking a man once he's down. Leave off with your fighting now," said the stranger.

The crowd began to complain. Some of them had bet a shilling or two that Chandler would whip young O'Hara, and they wanted to see the fighting finished.

The big man put his bag down and stood with his hands on his hips. He had a full red beard. His eyes squinted almost shut when he smiled. "Once a man's down, he's down. Anyone else caring to see the rest of a fight can be holding up his fists to me."

No one challenged the stranger. Grumbling about the spoiled fight, the watchers returned to their homes.

The big man bent down and lifted Devin upright. Then he bent down and picked up the white rabbit's foot, Devin's good luck charm. "Well, this won't be serving its purpose now, will it?" He handed the rabbit's foot to Devin.

Devin didn't say anything. He shrugged his shoulders and took the lucky charm from the man. He continued looking at the ground as he put it in his pocket.

The man pulled out a handkerchief to wipe the smeared blood on Devin's face. Devin turned his head away. In addition to the hurt in his stomach and face, he felt shame because Katey had seen him cry. If only once, just once, he could beat Paul, he would make Paul cry. Cry and cry.

Bebo came up to Devin. She licked his hand and whined as though she understood his pain.

"Have it your way," said the stranger. "Leave that blood there all over your face. You'll be giving your mother's heart a failure. Her thinking it's your whole face got busted off, not just a little skin here and there."

Devin said nothing. His mother would scold him for fighting, but she didn't know what it was like to be pushed by a bully. He turned back to the big man and noticed that there were white hairs growing amongst the red in the man's beard.

"Here now, let's have a look-see at what he's done." The big man held Devin's face gently in his large hand. He looked at the cut above Devin's eye, then reached to his belt and withdrew a leather drinking pouch. He uncorked it, lifted the pouch to his mouth, and took a long, hard drink. Whenever Devin's grandfather drank, his Adam's apple moved up and down like a ball in his throat. Devin wondered if the stranger's Adam's apple moved up and down too, but he couldn't see anything, for the stranger's neck was hidden by his red beard.

After the stranger swallowed, he poured some of the drink into his handkerchief and began to dab at Devin's face.

"You're a real little scrapper, is what you are. That lad was a whole lot bigger than you. But you was there, slugging away at him. You got lots of spirit, is what you've got." The big man touched his handkerchief to a cut on the left corner of Devin's mouth. It was a deep cut, and Devin pulled back from the cloth. The alcohol in the drink made the cut sting.

Katey interrupted now. "Paul Chandler always beats Devin. Won't let him alone."

"And what is it you'll be calling yourself?" the stranger asked.

"Devin."

"But Paul's always calling him shrimp," Katey added.

Devin, ashamed of his size, stared at a purply-gray, almost perfectly round stone the size of a plum that was on the ground.

Katey continued. "I'm Katey. I live next door to Devin. And this is Bebo," she added.

The big man reached down and patted Bebo, then looked up and said, "I'm Thomas Costello. And it's the top of the day that I'll be wishing to you and to the young lady here." The big man held out a huge hand.

Devin thought the hand looked as big as an anvil. If the man squeezed, he could crush Devin's fingers. Paul had done that to him once, grabbed Devin's hand in a pretend handshake — "Let's be friends, De-e-vin." Paul had squeezed his hand so hard, Devin's knuckles had cracked and felt as though they had broken, and Paul had laughed. Now Costello grabbed Devin's hand before he could think about refusing. And just as Costello had touched Devin's face with gentleness, so too, the handshake had the same quality. Costello's hand was calloused to such a point that Devin felt as though he were touching tree bark, but the pressure of the big fingers was gentle.

"So tell me, young Devin. How is it that you get to be fighting with someone who stands head and shoulders above where you'll be?"

Katey answered. "Paul Chandler is a ruffian. I hate him."

Devin met the stranger's gaze directly, and for the first time noticed that the stranger's left eyelid drooped over his eye, so that it looked as though the stranger was winking. "I saw a wolf," Devin said firmly.

"A wolf." The stranger pursed his lips. "You sure it was a wolf and not a dog that you was seeing?"

"It was a wolf," Devin said, his voice full of fight again.

"Easy there, lad. And take that look out of your eye, will you? You won't have to be fighting me like you did that Tom Farthing. But you're sure it was a wolf?"

"It was a wolf," Devin repeated.

"There ain't been no wolves seen around here for . . ." The stranger shook his head. "Years. . . . There's a bounty, you know. People get paid for killing 'em. Five shillings for the tails and ears of males and ten for a bitch. A man once could make a comfortable living hunting them. Done it meself in the past."

"It was this close." Devin reached out. "I could've touched it. It had yellow eyes. Paul didn't believe me. He shoved me, and then . . ." Devin looked at the ground again.

Katey, anxious not to be left out of the conversation, said, "Devin's birthday is on Hallow's Eve. But it's bad luck to be born on Hallow's Eve. So his grandmother rubbed him all over with goose grease, and she gave him his lucky rabbit's foot as a charm against the devil. My mother told me." Katey looked self-satisfied.

Devin was embarrassed.

The big man smiled. "A rabbit's foot might be useful against the devil, lad, but against a tuck duck like the Chandler you'll be needing more than just a bit o' good luck. You know, lad, once I was about the same size as what you are. Skinny, I was too, and like you, I had always a Tom Farthing, a cabbage brain, lead head, what was never letting me in peace. But one day, I got me own."

Devin looked at the big man. "Small like me?"

"You just ain't grown yet, lad. Look at your feet. Them ain't a small lad's feet."

"Did you beat him up?" Devin was excited now.

"I'll tell you what I did do. But first you have to tell me the way to the blacksmith shop."

"It's that way." Devin pointed. "Close to the butcher shop that Paul Chandler's father owns."

"You go home now, lad. Tomorrow you come to the blacksmith shop. In no time at all, we'll be fixing you up."

*t*he next evening, Devin made his way to the blacksmith shop and found Thomas Costello working at the forge. The fire in the furnace rose high and hot, and Costello's moving shadow loomed large on the walls. Costello, a giant, sweating brute, pulled a red-hot bar from the fire. He held the bar with one set of tongs and, with another set, bent the glowing hot iron as easily as though it were a piece of taffy. He laid down one pair of tongs, took up his hammer, and hammered out the shoe on the anvil, showering sparks onto the dirt floor. There was an easy, regular rhythm to Costello's hammering, and the ring of metal on metal was almost music to Devin.

The big man wore a leather blacksmith's apron, but underneath the apron, Costello was bare-chested. Sweat ran in a steady stream from his forehead, down his face and neck. And when Costello turned around, Devin saw that his back was a stream of sweat as well.

A horse was tied in the blacksmith shop, a scrawny, duff-colored nag with a long face, slack knees, and high, bony shoulders. Obviously it belonged to one of the farmers who rented land from Squire Watson.

Squire Watson demanded very high rents from his farmers, and because of the high rents they were extremely poor. At the end of each harvest, many of them had to give almost all their oats and wheat to him as payment for their land. Often, after the rents were paid, the peasant families had very little to eat all year long except potatoes and cabbages.

Devin liked horses. He went to the animal's side, petting its bony flank. Feeling sorry for it because it was so thin, he reached into his pocket, pulled out a small chunk of apple, and held it beneath the horse's velvet nose. The horse sniffed, blew air loudly from its nostrils, and then crunched the apple between its teeth.

Thomas looked up. "Top of the evening to you, lad. We'll be starting as soon as I'm done." He finished nailing the last shoe onto the horse's back hoof, then led the horse outside.

When he came back in, he unbuckled his blacksmith's apron, then wiped his forehead and chest and huge hands in a rag. Then he said, "Well now, laddie, stand up here in front o' me. Put up your fists, now!

No, not like that. Not in front o' your chest. In front o' your face." And the great, anvil-sized fist came out of nowhere.

Devin ducked, but it was too late. Costello's fist caught him under the chin, snapping his head back hard enough that Devin bit his tongue.

"Ouch!"

Costello punched Devin in the nose. Devin drew back. "I'm tired!" he shouted, but Costello's big, relentless fist was there again, lightly hitting the side of his face.

Devin turned his back on Costello. "I'm tired," he repeated, "and my arms hurt. I don't want to fight anymore."

"Tell that to the Chandler the next time he comes after you. You know what the Chandler will be doing when you turn your back? He'll be kicking you in the pants," and Costello did exactly that, knocking Devin face down onto the packed earth.

"And then you know what the Chandler will be doing, don't you?" Costello was now standing beside Devin, and he could see the big, wide, rough, scuffed toes of Costello's shoes, just as he had seen Chandler's shoes. "Answer me, lad. What does the Chandler do when you're down?"

Costello bent down, grabbed Devin by the shoulders, and lifted him to standing. "He kicks you in the face or in the stomach. Ain't that right, me lad?"

Devin looked at the floor. He sniffled and nodded.

Then Thomas laid his big arm on Devin's shoulders and spoke more gently. "You're quick, lad, but you won't be having much stamina, or much strength."

Devin sniffled again. "What's stamina?" he asked, still looking at the ground.

"Staying power, lad. So as your body can be doing what it's got to be doing, but doing it for a long time. You got to be taking some vigorous air each day. You'll be staying soft as me granny's backside with the work what you'll be doing. Working in a tavern. Serving up ale and cabbages. That'll never give you muscles, lad. The butcher's boy, he's strong and big as he is 'cause he'll be helping his father lifting and hauling the carcasses of cows and sheep. It'll be taking you a little time to be getting up some strength."

For the first time since Costello had knocked him down, Devin looked at him. "How do you know?"

"I come from a family of fifteen children, and me the seventh from the oldest. Me brothers was always picking on me. And then one summer, me father put me to work, picking rocks up in the field to be building stone fences. Me brothers was older and went off to France to be fighting in the war against the English. I was about your age, I was, and too young to be fighting.

"Well, by the end of the summer, lad, I had shoulders on me twice as big as before and arms too.

"Well, the lease ran out on me father's property, so we had to move on.

"I was a lad like you then, and a certain Michael Patrick O'Flaherty, who came from the south, was holding a boxing match in the streets of Sligo. 'Hey you, lad,' he was saying to me, 'fetch me a drink.' And after the fight, O'Flaherty asked me father what he would be asking for me to work for him. Me father had no home then, and eight other children and me mother to care for, so he sold me to O'Flaherty for five shillings and a promise he would treat me good."

Costello scratched his beard. "Well, you see, lad, O'Flaherty, to keep up his strength, would run every day. Two big iron weights in his hands and he'd run with them, oh, four, sometimes five miles. I started running with him. O'Flaherty was getting older and I was growing up. And I started boxing too.

"Thomas Brian Costello. I got meself known all through the western counties. Wasn't a man what could beat me. I could knock down anybody. Even the English soldiers. A man can make a fine living as a boxer. Spectators will be cheering the winner and tossing him all manner of coins and money. More than he knows what to do with. But time being what time is, it changes a man. Just as time will be making the likes o' you," and he pointed at Devin, "grow bigger, so it'll be making a man grow older. A crowd loves a man when he's winning, and they'll be cheering him on.

But when he's losing," Thomas shrugged, "well, they'll be cursing him and insulting him. Calling him a dog's vomit, throwing rotten apples at him, all kinds of filth. So, when I stopped winning at boxing, I decided to come this way. Find a new place to live. A blacksmith can always be using a strong arm to help him. And so here I be."

After the first lesson with Costello, Devin began running. Every day he ran along the road through Barne's Gap, and every night he went to the blacksmith shop for another boxing session.

One night, after three weeks, Costello praised him. "You're quick, lad, and you're getting stronger by the day. In no time at all, you'll be showing the Chandler where to be sticking his marbles."

❧ 6 ❧

Devin was carrying two large stones in his hands as he ran. They were heavy and his arms and fingers ached with holding them, but Devin was determined he was going to get stronger. Bebo ran just behind him, nipping at his heels, Katey followed, running slightly behind.

They were running along the road that cut through Barne's Gap, and they were headed north along the gap in the direction of the Glenelly River. It was a warm, moist day. Spring had flowered, and the air was filled with the sweet, green smell of newly budded leaves and white thorn blossoms.

Suddenly a noise came through the forest. Devin stopped so quickly that Bebo's nose collided with the backs of his knees, and Katey, who was just a couple of steps behind, tripped over Bebo and tumbled to the ground. Squire Watson's hounds were baying at the hunt.

Devin and Katey had both been warned to stay away from Squire Watson when he was hunting. A big-bellied man with a ham-hock face, he was a fanatic and a drinker. He would trample without care over the newly planted fields of his tenants or through their yards, running down chickens, piglets, dogs, whatever got in his way. He always rode like a madman, thinking of nothing except the animal that he chased. He would wave the tail of a dead fox as though it were the captured flag of an enemy.

Almost every day he thundered through Scotch Town, his pack of hounds around him. His dogs were wiry-haired, rawboned creatures, almost as big as calves, with brambly, coarse coats.

But his horses were sleek, splendid animals, and they were beautiful and exciting to see as they galloped across the fields and through the forest. And even though Devin had been warned, he never missed an opportunity to look at them.

Devin threw down the stones and he and Katey and Bebo ran into the forest in the direction of the hunt. They ran as fast as they could toward the howling, baying hounds. Branches slapped at their eyes and grabbed at their sleeves as they swerved and darted around trees and shrubs and fallen logs.

The excited baying came from the left. Even in this

short space of time, the dogs had advanced rapidly. A hill rose in front of Devin and Katey. If they didn't hurry, the hounds would pass on the other side and disappear.

The howling now grew frantic. Already breathless, Devin ran faster. As he crossed the top of the hill, he saw that the hounds had a wolf in chase.

When Devin saw the gray-black coat, he knew immediately that it was the same wolf he had seen in the mist.

A steep rise of stone blocked the fleeing creature's path. The wolf leaped up the incline, but just as it did so, one of the hounds clamped the wolf's hind leg in its jaws.

The wolf was pulled down amidst the pack of hounds and, with its back to the stone, turned to face the pack. Again Devin saw the blaze of yellow eyes.

Up to now, Devin hadn't thought whether the animal was male or female. It had simply been a terrifying, frightening, huge, gray-black wolf with yellow eyes. When it reared up battling the dogs, Devin saw the teats where it had suckled its young, and he realized that this was a mother wolf.

Two hounds grabbed at the animal's shoulder, one on each side, and they pulled her down so that she was fighting on her side. Another hound grabbed hold of her flank and ripped back, pulling away a chunk of fur and flesh. But the wolf, at the same time, managed to grab a hound's foot in her powerful jaws and crush the paw. The hound yowled and jumped back, its foot hanging uselessly in the air.

Somehow the wolf managed to get to her feet, but her hindquarters were dragging badly. Hounds circled from three sides, all of them snarling, lips pulled back, showing slavering, ugly fangs.

Devin was horrified and confused. He had been told by his grandfather that wolves ripped men and children apart, but this wolf had done nothing to him. He had been told that wolves were monsters, indestructible as the mountains themselves, but this wolf, bloodied, limp, and lame, looked like a small old woman fighting desperately for her life.

Another hound sunk its teeth into the wolf's face just under her eye, and ripped. Now there was blood all over the wolf's face as well as her body. Devin didn't know how many hounds there were. All he knew was that the fight was unfair. He picked up a large stone and hurled it.

Devin was a good shot; the hound let out a yelp and let go of the wolf. But as soon as that hound let go, another one attached. Devin bent again and found another rock, and then a stick, and he hurled them both. There were at least a dozen hounds. And Devin picked up another rock and then another, and still another, and let fly with each of them. Then Katey was grabbing rocks, and soon the air was filled with stones and pebbles and rocks, as both threw rocks as fast as they could. And Bebo barked furiously.

Squire Watson galloped up, pulling back so brutally on the reins that his horse slid on its haunches, nearly collapsing.

The squire dismounted and drew his fowling piece. He stuffed powder and shot into the front of the barrel, then lifted the musket to his shoulder.

Devin saw the squire take aim and raced at him, throwing himself against the man's legs. The squire was startled from the impact and didn't shoot.

"Why, you Irish cur. . . . I'll teach you to . . ." The squire hit Devin so hard across the face that he flew to the ground.

The squire took aim again, the shiny wooden butt of his gun pressed against his shoulder, the black steel barrel pointed directly at the wolf. The loud, quick clap of gunfire sounded.

For a split second, nothing happened. The wolf had her teeth in the neck of an almost pure white dog, but then the white dog was suddenly loose. The wolf dropped to one knee as though she were going to lie down. She tried to stand again, and for a moment it seemed as though she would succeed, for she managed to get the bent leg straight and to take a step, but in taking that step she crumpled. One leg twitched slightly, then stilled.

A second man, a dog handler, leaped off his horse and began to pull the hounds from the dead animal. Squire Watson walked ponderously toward the wolf. He bent and lifted its bleeding, limp body.

Devin tried not to cry. Big boys don't cry, his mother always said, but he couldn't help it now. His faced ached where Squire Watson had struck him, but that wasn't the reason he cried. He cried because the wolf he had seen that day the mist had fallen down the mountain, that proud, storm-colored, yellow-eyed animal, was dead. This time, Devin didn't try to hide his tears from Katey; she was crying too.

The squire talked with his houndsman. "This bitch will bring us a handsome bounty. Ten shillings, the treasury is paying."

The houndsman answered, nodding in the direction from which the wolf had run, "And by her looks, she's got a litter somewheres."

"Probably the mate of the one we killed before," Squire Watson said. "I swear, those yellow eyes belong to the devil himself. I won't rest so long as one of these hellish creatures is left anywhere. The hounds have had enough of the hunt today. Tomorrow we'll find the den and destroy the pups. Fiendish beasts!" He dropped the wolf and shouted at Devin and Katey.

"Damned meddlesome curs! Don't ever let me see you where I'm hunting again, or I'll have your Irish carcasses whipped and thrown in jail for trespassing." And for emphasis, he pointed his musket at them. "Away with you now!"

7

Devin and Katey ran from Squire Watson. When they thought they were far enough away, they stopped running and began to walk. They didn't speak, and their eyes no longer looked up or out at the sky or at the trees, but were cast down.

Mist appeared to be seeping up out of the forest floor. A spider had woven a web between two sprigs of fern and a butterfly had been caught in the silken trap. The haze reached out with silent fingers, curled against the web, floated into it, but unlike the butterfly the mist floated out again.

Devin couldn't stop thinking about the wolf, how she had continued to fight even when severely wounded, how slack her body had gone after she had been shot. She had looked invincible that day in the ravine, her yellow eyes blazing through the fog.

When Devin finally looked up he realized that the mist had silently engulfed them. It had risen high into the uppermost branches and seemed to hang there amongst the leaves.

"Come on, Katey," he said, taking her hand. "Let's go home."

"Devin, I'm scared," she said quietly. "What happens if a dullahan comes?"

Devin didn't want Katey to know he was frightened too. "They can't come into the forest. There's no room for the coach wheels to go through the trees."

But Katey had a different story about dullahans. "My mother says that they can go anywhere the fog goes. A ghost coach can even come in under the door, she says, same as what the fog does."

At this moment, Bebo pricked up her ears and barked a sharp, quick bark.

Katey jumped closer to Devin. He felt the hair on the back of his neck rise. He had heard something as well. Bebo spun around and chased off into the woods.

"Bebo! Bebo! Come back!" Katey yelled. But all the children saw was Bebo's white tail disappearing into the mist.

Katey ran after her dog.

Devin shouted for them both, but the mist was

growing thicker, and he couldn't see either the girl or the dog. He had to follow Katey's voice as she called after Bebo. Tree branches in the fog grew long and clawlike, grabbing at Devin's hair and clothes. The grass and stones and underforest were slippery. For balance, Devin reached out his hand, grabbing a rough tree trunk. He touched something wet and slimy, drew his hand back immediately; toadstools, moist with fog, grew in the crotch of the tree.

Steps came through the mist. Branches crackled underfoot. Grass swished as something moved through it. "Katey," he called. "Is that you?" But the thing that was moving toward him didn't answer. It was moving zigzag. Devin felt the terror of the unseen thing coming toward him. "Katey, where are you?" he shouted. Still no answer. Only that thing coming toward him. He tried to turn and run, but his legs wouldn't move. His body wouldn't move. His heart sounded as though it were beating in two parts, one on either side of his head, beating against his ears like drums, louder and louder, and behind his eyeballs, echoing and echoing.

And then a furry thing shot out at him from the mist. Devin yelled, but he stopped in midvoice, for the furry thing was Bebo, coming to him in excitement, her tongue and paws eager. Her fur, damp from the mist, smelled of something — something wild.

Devin bent down to Bebo and stroked her silky ears.

Her fur was covered with small bits of wood rot and dust. There were bits of wood across the bridge of her nose and in her thick white ruff.

Devin patted her, but she was shedding and his hands became covered with big chunks of moist dog hair. He rubbed his hands together to get rid of the hair, and as he did so, Bebo scooted off again.

"Bebo! Devin! Where are you?" Katey called as she appeared, her wheat-colored hair shimmering and moist, her round face glistening with a veil of mist.

"She's found something," Katey said, "but I don't know what. She was gone before I could find her."

Now they both called Bebo, their voices strangely muffled in the mist.

"She wouldn't have found a dullahan?" asked Katey hesitantly.

"Dogs don't like ghosts. She wouldn't have gone back there."

They continued calling and whistling.

Bebo came bounding up, her snout covered with more wood chips and dust. She jumped excitedly at Katey's knees, then was off again.

A breeze came and lifted the mist, lifted it in a momentary wave above the ground. Katey and Devin saw Bebo with her head stuck in the end of a fallen tree trunk. But the breeze died and the fog blanketed the ground once more.

As Devin and Katey approached, they heard small,

sharp growling sounds. Bebo was crouched down at one end of the log, her head thrust into it.

Katey called, and Bebo pulled her head out of the log.

Devin bent down to look inside the trunk. He bent down very slowly, frightened of what he might see.

Bebo excitedly shoved her face into the hollow log again, so Devin got a face full of wet dog fur. "Bebo!" he sputtered.

Katey grabbed her dog around the neck, and she and Devin cautiously lowered their faces to the dead tree trunk and peered inside. The tree trunk was the entrance to a den dug in the hillside. Inside were three wolf puppies, three furry, clumsy puppies, chewing on one another's tails and paws and tumbling in rough play.

Katey and Devin looked at each other, and although neither of them spoke, each knew what the other was thinking. Each of them was thinking of the squire's words. *The hounds have had enough of the hunt today. Tomorrow we'll find the den and destroy the pups.*

❧ 8 ❧

*T*here were two female puppies and a male. The male was dark and gray like a storm cloud. It was for this reason that Devin called him Sdhoirm, which in Irish means "storm." Katey named the other two puppies Dun, which means "brown," and Beg, which means "small." Kneeling on the ground, neither Katey nor Devin could stop petting and playing with the puppies. Katey kept saying over and over again that they were adorable. Like all puppies, the little wolves loved to play. But their teeth were needle sharp, and when they chewed on fingers with happy but too fierce enthusiasm, Devin and Katey yelped with pain.

"They're hungry," said Katey, rubbing at the place where Dun's teeth had broken the skin on her palm.

It was late afternoon. Devin had a small crust of

bread in his pocket left over from his breakfast, and he fed it to Beg because she was the smallest. Immediately Sdhoirm pounced on Beg and snatched the bread from her.

"You're such a bully!" exclaimed Devin. "Leave something for your sister." He grabbed the bread, broke it in two, and gave one morsel to Beg and the other to Sdhoirm.

"What about Dun?" Katey asked. "She must be hungry too."

As if in answer, Dun began to whimper, her clear blue eyes looking first at Katey and than at Devin. She jumped at Devin, trying to lick his face, as if she were asking to be fed.

"They were probably waiting for the mother to bring back food to them," said Devin. He searched through his pockets for another crust of bread. He turned them inside out, but they were empty.

From Devin's grandfather, they had both heard the story of the Eagle's Nest. An Irish prince and princess were taken away to the mountains by a faithful servant so they wouldn't be captured by the invading English. In the mountains, the old servant fell and died, and the young prince and princess were near starvation. They were seen by two eagles who flew over and dropped food to them and helped the children grow up. Devin and Katey decided that they would look after the puppies, just as the eagles had looked after the prince and princess. They planned to bring some food for the puppies and move them to the mountains on the north side of the Glenelly River, where they would be safe.

Devin and Katey ran back to town as quickly as they could. At the edge of town, they split up so no one would suspect anything. Katey went first, and Devin watched her run down the main road. Her pigtails flew behind her as she ran, and her skirts billowed about her knees. He hoped no one would see her. The fog was less thick here than it had been in the forest.

Devin continued on behind the houses to the south side of Scotch Town. The mill, the butcher shop, and the blacksmith shop were all close to the Owenkillew River. Devin never liked coming this way, for he always worried about Paul Chandler. But this was the shortest way home.

As Devin walked, he heard the regular, solid ring of Thomas Costello's hammer. He wanted to share his excitement about the wolf pups, but he remembered that Costello had hunted wolves. No, this had to be a secret between himself and Katey.

Devin passed close to the river where the great moss-covered wheel of the flour mill turned and turned endlessly in the current. The wooden wheel squeaked and groaned as water splashed through its paddles. This was where the farmers brought their oats to be ground into flour. And it was here that Devin brought the grain for his family's cow to be ground. His mother would make him milk the cow when he got home. And he would have other chores. He was overcome with a sense of urgency and began to run.

A sudden, sharp pain in his shin made him cry out and stop. A rock caught him in the right shoulder. Another caught him on the arm.

Paul Chandler swaggered out from behind the corner of the mill. "You're a sly dog, Shrimp O'Hara. I seen you coming back with Katey the cow." There was a hard, dangerous look on his face. In his left hand he held a slingshot, which was drawn back and ready to shoot again. Sean and Jimmy were with him.

Jimmy came to Devin's defense. "Leave him be, Paul. Let's rub off."

"Shut up, Jimmy," Paul said, then turned to Devin. "What were you doing?"

Devin didn't want to fight with Paul. He wanted to be left alone so he could get food for the wolf cubs and get them moved. He could see a spot of black between one of Paul's bottom teeth and his gum where his teeth were beginning to rot.

"Not your concern." Devin turned to walk away from Paul.

"Answer me, runt." Paul Chandler grabbed Devin by the shoulder to make Devin face him again. "What do you and Katey the cow do?"

"He's smaller than you," Jimmy said to Paul.

"Yeah, but he thinks he's bigger. Don't you, shrimp? Sean! Dig up some worms." Paul turned back to Devin. "Think you're big since Costello came to town?" Paul shoved Devin.

Devin shoved back, and the boys just stood in front of each other, glaring.

"Wanna eat some worms, worm?" Paul sneered.

"Eat 'em yourself, worm. It's your name."

"Sean, hurry up!"

"Can't find any."

"Turn up the stones, stupid!" Paul ordered. He sneered at Devin. "Think you're big, shrimp puke?"

"Got some. Couple of big, fat ones," said Sean, and holding the gray, slimy-looking worms in his fingers, he approached.

"Now, Jimmy, we're going to see some fun. Come here, worm puke, and eat your dinner."

"Eat it yourself, Chandler. My name doesn't mean worm."

Paul went at Devin, his fists flying, but Devin hit him with two well-placed punches: the first to his jaw, the second to the tenderest part of his stomach.

Wailing with pain, Paul dropped to his knees.

"Hit him again," Jimmy cried.

For revenge's sake, Devin wanted to hit Paul. He wanted to hit him for all the times Paul had beaten him up, blackened his eyes, bruised his arms, made him cry. Devin wanted to hit Paul again and again and again. But Costello's words were in the back of his mind. *Never hit a man once he's down.*

Sean stood close to the two boys now. "I got the worms," he said, dangling one from his fingers.

"Yeah, make *him* eat worms," Jimmy said. "His name is Chandler."

But Costello's words were still there. Devin turned and walked past the mill slowly. Then he began to run. Jimmy followed him.

Paul sat up and shouted, "Jimmy, come back here!" But Jimmy continued running after Devin. Only Sean was left, looking happily at the worms as he lifted them from one muddy hand to another. "Throw those down, you stupid retard!" yelled Paul as he watched Devin growing smaller in the distance. "I'll get you back, runt puke!" he shouted after Devin. "I'll get you back!"

9

Devin only stopped running when he reached the front of his house. Jimmy caught up with him.

"Can I come inside your house?" Jimmy asked. "I'll let you use my slingshot."

Devin was cautious and answered simply that he wasn't staying home.

"You can't keep playing with a girl," said Jimmy.

Jimmy's mother came out of his house and called him to come inside.

Jimmy glared at his mother, who was waving her arm for him to come. He waited for Devin to say something. When he didn't, Jimmy held out his slingshot. "You can use it," he said.

Rubbing the toe of his shoe across a stone, Devin looked at the ground. He ignored the slingshot.

When Devin didn't answer him, Jimmy said, "Well, I'd better be rubbing off, I guess." He turned slowly and left.

The house in which Devin lived with his parents was owned by Devin's grandfather. Devin remembered how, when he was four or five years old, the cow and chickens were kept in the stable that was built directly onto the end of the house. To the Irish, it was considered good luck to keep the cow where she could see the fire, but the English travelers didn't like to see animals in the same room in which they slept. Devin's mother persuaded her father to turn the stable into a lodging room. Devin's father, who worked in a quarry cutting stones on the outskirts of Scotch Town, had built another stable some yards away from the house.

At first Devin's grandfather had helped with the tavern, but now mostly he sat by the fire in a huge chair carved out of a solid piece of oak. He smoked bitter-smelling stuff in his pipe and told story after story. Devin's mother ran the tavern, and it was Devin's responsibility to help her.

The tavern was called the Black Boar Tavern. Because some people couldn't read, a large wooden sign picturing a black boar's head hung above the door. A horseshoe was nailed just above the front door to bring good luck to the house. Another horseshoe was nailed on the door of the cow stable. Up to now, the horseshoes had worked. The O'Haras weren't rich, but they were much better off than the farmers who rented land from Squire Watson, or the beggars who came to the tavern asking for food.

There was no chimney in the tavern. The hearth was located in the center of the room. Since Devin's family burned peat, which gave off no sparks, it was not necessary to have a chimney. The fire was kept low and the smoke rose into the upper rafters and circulated between the thatch. The smoke kept mice and birds and wasps from nesting in the thatch and destroying it. The peat gave off a sweet smell, a grassy, aromatic smell.

In the back corner of the house, far from the fire, moss grew because of the dampness. But close to the pink-blue glow of the turf fire, with the rain running off the thatch on a cold winter's night and his grandfather telling story after story — there was no other place in the world that Devin would rather be.

The floor of the tavern was hard, pressed dirt. The sleeping area was to the right of the hearth, the eating and drinking area to the left. Devin's parents slept in a wooden bed that Devin's grandfather had carved, and Devin slept on the floor on a straw mat covered with a quilt made of goose feathers. Papli always slept sitting up in his big oak chair. He had phlegmy lungs, and if he lay down he couldn't breathe very well.

The furniture in the eating space was low, and consisted of three benches lining the walls and three tables. Against one wall was a large oak vat where the ale was kept.

Devin's mother cooked in large, three-legged metal pots that stood in the turf coals. When Devin walked in, she was standing with her back to him, stirring a pot of stew.

"And where is it that you've been all afternoon?"

"Nowhere," he answered.

"Nowhere, is it? Well then, will you be telling me how it is that you're covered with brambles and grass?" She approached him and brushed her hand down his sleeve. "Is it fighting you've been again?" she asked.

He shrugged.

"The Chandler? Why don't you be leaving the likes of him alone?"

"I beat him," Devin said excitedly. "I hit him and I . . ."

"And wasn't Jesus telling us not to be fighting?"

"Jesus didn't have a bully like Paul Chandler!"

"Devin, Devin, what am I going to do with you? You'll get yourself killed one of these days because of that boy."

"But he won't beat me anymore. Thomas showed me how to do it."

"And there's another without sense. Thomas Costello. A grown man showing you how to use fists."

There were more urgent things to be taken care of.

Devin changed the subject. "Have you any table scraps or bones?"

"And what is it that you'll be needing those for?"

Devin had planned what he was going to say. "Bebo."

"There's a bone in the cupboard. But mind, you've got to be milking the cow before."

"Can't I do it later? Katey said that Bebo's very hungry."

"And by the looks of Bebo, it won't be hurting her to be hungry from time to time. Round and fat like a piggy's bottom, she is."

"I need it now. I promised Katey."

"Devin! You'll milk the cow, and right away, or I'll be telling your father when he comes home. He won't be as goodly natured as me. I have to be going to see Molly Flannagan. She's under the weather. And when I come back, I expect to be seeing that you've finished." She handed him a wooden pail.

Devin's heart jumped at this news of his mother's absence. He made a big show of taking the pail and allowing it to bang against his leg as he walked. But he didn't go into the cow shed. From the stable he wouldn't be able to see his mother leave.

Waiting for her to go, he hid behind the back corner of the house and put down the pail. He pressed his face against the cool, rough stones and traced their square and rectangular patterns with his fingers. He would take the bone and meet Katey as soon as his mother left. He would milk the cow when he came back.

What was his mother doing? What was taking her so long? She always told him to hurry. Hurry, hurry, hurry! But did *she* ever hurry? No! Never! She always took as long as she wanted. It wasn't fair.

A spider, a daddy long legs, was slowly crawling up the wall of the house. The spider reached out with one fine, long leg, and then another.

Devin put his hand in front of the spider, and the spider stopped momentarily. It lifted one thin leg onto Devin's index finger. Then another. The spider was on the first knuckle of Devin's finger.

Something touched Devin's ear.

He screamed and jumped nearly three feet into the air, spinning around as he did so, sending the pail to the ground in a terrible clatter.

His mother was standing there. "And just what in the name of heaven and all the stars do you think you'll be doing here?"

"Nothing," he said.

"Devin," she said. "The good Lord knows I'll be losing patience with you. Now milk that cow!"

"What are you doing here?" he asked her.

"I was coming to hang clothes on the line when I saw you sneaking about here."

"I was trying to catch a spider," he said, as he looked

for it. "It was here a minute ago. You scared it away." He gave his mother a belligerent look.

Katey came running up to the side of the house.

"You can be going and getting the bone from the pantry just as soon as Mr. Smart Breeches finishes his work," Devin's mother said. "Now go and be tending to it before I lose me patience with the both of you."

Devin gave his mother a sullen look, but he took up the pail and carried it to the stable. As he pulled open the door, it creaked horrendously.

This was a job that Devin was supposed to have done a long time ago: rub the hinges of the door with bacon fat so they didn't squeak anymore. But Devin always forgot. Now he gave the door another angry pull and made it squeak even louder. The good luck horseshoe nailed onto the stable door banged loudly against the wood.

Branwen, the cow, was already in the stable. She was light brown with big, liquid eyes, gentle and curious as her disposition.

Branwen mooed gently. Devin knew this was her way of saying that she was happy to see him.

Normally Devin did things in the stable in a certain order. He would first go to Branwen and talk to her and pet her forehead with its curly mat of hair that felt like tiny, soft springs. He would then tie her to the manger, brush her, and milk her, singing songs and talking to her as he did so.

Branwen was not a wild cow. He tied her only because if he didn't she would turn and lick him right in the face after she had finished eating. This was her way of saying thank you, and her way of saying I love you. But a cow's tongue is huge and rough, about a hundred times rougher than a cat's tongue. To Devin, being licked by Branwen was like being hit in the face with a sandbag. Devin loved Branwen, but he didn't like it when she licked him.

Today Devin was in a hurry, and he didn't pet Branwen's forehead or scratch her behind the ears. Instead he quickly bent down into the manger and grabbed for the length of rope. Devin's sweater crawled up his back, exposing a couple of inches of bare flesh.

Branwen, always ready to show her affection, licked Devin as hard as she could on his bare back. Devin yelled loudly and dropped the rope back into the manger. "That hurts!" he scolded, rubbing at his back.

Branwen got a glum, sad look in her large, purple cow eyes, and she turned her head away from Devin. He immediately wrapped his arms around her head and scratched her behind the ears. "Sorry," he said. "I didn't mean to hurt your feelings, but your tongue's for eating grass, not for kissing people." He rubbed at his back one more time.

He tied her, then stroked her neck and shoulder and her rump, and then went to the oat bin to get her some food.

He fed her something called chop, a mixture of ground oats and some salt and bran. Chop was very itchy and dusty, but Branwen loved it. She plunged her nose into it, then lifted her head high into the air and closed her purple eyes and chewed with pleasure, her sandbag tongue turning happily in her mouth.

Afraid that his mother would hear, Devin and Katey had not talked during this time. Finally Katey asked him, "What is it you wanted a bone for?"

"What do you think, silly?" Devin was beginning to rethink the whole maneuver of moving the puppies with the help of a girl. Jimmy had embarrassed him. *You can't keep playing with a girl,* he had said, his freckled nose crinkled up as though he had smelled something very bad.

"Silly yourself," Katey said.

"I'm not as big a silly as you are," Devin shot back. He grabbed the milk stool and sat down beside Branwen. "I wanted a bone for the wolf cubs," he said.

The milk stool was a short, crude three-legged stool with a round seat. Devin's grandfather had carved it and put it together.

"You are so a silly," Katey said. "Anyone who would want to take bones to pups is a silly." She came and stood behind Branwen, watching Devin milk.

Devin placed the pail so that it was under Branwen's udder. At the same time, he tucked his head in the space just behind her round stomach in front of her hind leg. It was a warm, hollow space, and when he tucked his head there he could hear the gentle swishings and sloshings of Branwen's stomach as she chewed.

"They have to eat something," Devin said. He grabbed hold of Branwen's two back teats and began to milk her. Her teats were plump with milk. They were about the size of an adult's fingers. The skin was smooth and hairless, unlike the udder itself, which was covered in fine, short white hair. As Devin pulled down first one teat and then the other, the first spurt of milk made a spssh sound as it hit the bottom of the empty pail. Spssh, spsssh, each time followed by a softer wooden echo, and then the bottom of the pail was no longer empty and the sound of the milk streaming into it changed into a frothy, liquid sound.

"Don't you know anything?" Katey criticized. "Puppies can't eat bones, silly. They need soft food."

"Your head is soft," Devin said, and aiming a teat at Katey, he sprayed her in the face with a stream of milk.

"Devin! Don't!" Katey wiped at the milk with her hands. Annoyed, she sat down on the low partition that divided Branwen's stall from the rest of the stable. "That's what puppies need, silly," she said disdainfully. "Milk, not bones."

"They do so need bones. How do you think their teeth grow strong? It's by chewing on bones."

"All their baby teeth fall out. The same way yours did when you were small. So there, silly."

"If you're so smart, why are you sitting up there?" asked Devin.

"What else am I supposed to be doing? Standing there so you can spray me with milk again, spider-brain?"

"No, spider-brain, you could come and help me and we'd be done faster."

❧10❧

Devin and Katey had ladled some milk into a leather flask. From the tavern they had gathered gristle and fat and put them into a pouch, then scooted quickly and secretly out of town.

Now Katey poured the milk into a dish, but the wolflings refused to drink it. Instead they insistently tried to lick Katey's and Devin's faces.

Katey squealed. "Why do they always try to lick us?"

Not knowing the answer, Devin thought about Katey's question as he dumped the contents of the pouch. When the puppies devoured the gristle and fat and began to gnaw vigorously on the bone, he understood what all the licking meant. "They're wolves," Devin said matter-of-factly. "They eat meat. Their mother must have brought them food in her mouth."

Even after the cubs had chewed the bone bare, they

refused to drink the milk. Instead they licked at the food smells and tastes that clung to Devin's and Katey's hands and continued to try and lick their cheeks and mouths. Sdhoirm's small pink tongue tickled Devin's neck and chin.

"They're already weaned," Devin said. "We'll have to bring more meat for them."

It was time to move the puppies. Devin put the bone back in the pouch. He picked up Sdhoirm and Dun, holding one in each arm. Katey carried Beg. In Devin's arms the pups squirmed and tumbled and growled — not at him, but at the gray wooden buttons on his wool sweater, which they tried to chew off. They growled and chewed and pulled. But their attention was soon caught by something else, and they began to chew on Devin's collar, then his ears.

"Ouch!" cried Devin, rubbing his ears. He lowered his arms so Sdhoirm couldn't reach so high. The pup went back to chewing on the sweater buttons, and when he tired of these he began chewing Dun's tail. But she snapped down on his nose and sent him whimpering into the hollow of Devin's neck just under his chin, where he remained with his wet, cool nose hidden until Devin and Katey came to the Glenelly River.

At the crossing the Glenelly River was shallow and narrow. Devin and Katey stopped on the edge, put the puppies down on the ground, and removed their shoes so they wouldn't get wet.

Dun found a stick and began to growl as he chewed on it. Beg sat down on her haunches and nipped at a flea. She scratched her ear with a hind paw. When she finished, she tilted her head to one side and looked at Katey and Devin with a puzzled expression that seemed to say, *Why are you doing that?* Sdhoirm found a fat black beetle that was crawling along the ground. He pounced on the bug and, snapping his jaws, quickly ate it in one swallow.

"Bebo doesn't eat bugs," said Katey.

"He's a hunter," Devin answered. "Bebo's not."

Sdhoirm noticed one of Devin's shoes lying on the ground and attacked it. Inside the shoe, he found a wonderful thing to chew on. He found Devin's knee sock.

"Hey," shouted Devin. "Give me my stocking."

But Sdhoirm wasn't giving up, and he yanked harder, growling ferociously and shaking his head from side to side as Devin tugged from the other end.

Devin tried gently to pry open the puppy's jaws, but Sdhoirm bit his knuckles, breaking the skin. Devin cried out and pulled his finger away. He hadn't realized how much stronger the jaw pressure of a wolfling was than that of a tame puppy. The wolflings looked like puppies, so Devin had assumed they were alike. In their playful attitude, they were similar, but their teeth were much sharper and stronger than a dog's teeth.

Sdhoirm still held the sock. Devin recalled how Dun had bitten down on Sdhoirm's muzzle, making him let go when he chewed on her tail. Devin pinched his fingers down firmly on the male wolf's nose. Immediately Sdhoirm let go of the sock.

They crossed the river carefully. On the other side, several hundred yards from the river, Devin and Katey found a shallow cave. They put the pups in the cave with the bone. Then Katey and Devin built up the front with sticks and twigs so that the pups couldn't get out.

Each time Katey or Devin picked up a stick, Bebo, ready to play, barked and wagged her tail excitedly. Sometimes Devin and Katey would throw a stick for her. She would bring it back and drop it at their feet, then yap and jump impatiently until the stick was thrown again.

The next day, when Squire Watson raced through the village with his huntsmen and his pack of hounds yapping and barking around his horse, Katey and Devin secretly looked at each other.

"Do you think the puppies are all right?" Katey whispered to Devin.

"Yes," he said. "Hounds can't smell anything if it crosses the river." Nonetheless, he was worried as well, and the two children snuck away from the village and headed for Barne's Gap. They crossed the Glenelly River and raced up to the puppies' new home. They peeped in behind the branches and both their hearts stopped.

"Devin!" cried Katey. "They're gone!" There was nothing but emptiness and a bare bone where the puppies should have been.

Devin and Katey listened, but heard nothing. No growling. No whining. Nothing except the *raawk* of a raven in a nearby tree.

Then something gray moved in the back of the cave, and Dun staggered forward sleepily, her mouth open in a huge yawn. She put her head down on her front paws and stretched and stretched. She began to whimper when she saw Devin and Katey. Beg came out into the sunlight right behind her.

But Sdhoirm was nowhere. Devin crawled into the cave and whistled and called, and still Sdhoirm didn't come. And then Katey saw a shadow of black beneath a bush.

"He's here, Devin!" She lifted up the puppy. Sdhoirm immediately started chewing on the red ribbons that tied her braids.

"Oh, stop!" she scolded. "You're naughty! Naughty! You'll get lost!"

"He must've dug out. We'll have to pile the branches better this time," said Devin.

The children fed the puppies with more bread and meat scraps and a couple of fish that Devin had snitched from the breakfast table.

As Katey and Devin played, they listened for the baying of Squire Watson's hounds. Once Katey looked up suddenly, thinking that she heard them. But they were far away on the other side of the river. For a while, the hounds came closer. Both Devin and Katey were ready to pick up the pups and run with them up onto the mountainside if they had to, but then the dog voices grew more distant until they faded completely.

Devin hugged the puppies and smothered his face in their fur. "You're safe now! All of you are safe. We'll protect you."

❧ 11 ❧

Over the next several weeks, the wolf cubs grew at a remarkable rate. At the tavern Devin was on a constant lookout for food to secret away for them. At first he was content to take scraps of gristle and bones and dried-out crusts of bread, but as the puppies grew, they required greater quantities of food. The children had to fish and to trap mice for them.

Three things didn't change over the next several weeks. The first was that no matter how much food Devin and Katey provided, the pups were always hungry. The second was that no matter how many branches or twigs they put in front of the den, Sdhoirm always found a way out. They had to look for him every day. The third was that Devin and Katey had to go to school two mornings a week, even though it was summertime.

Devin hated school. He hated sitting on some stupid, hard chair for what seemed like hours and hours, and he hated the school teacher, Master O'Grady. Master O'Grady was old and bent and he walked with a cane; he always wore a scarf around his neck, even in summertime, and he constantly hiccoughed. He had knobbly, wrinkly, ugly hands covered with brown spots and big veins that looked like worms. But the worst thing about Master O'Grady was his breath. It stank. It smelled like a barrel of rotting crow meat. He would bend over Devin's table and breathe on him while Devin tried to spell out words. And then he would grab Devin's ears and yank them if he made a mistake in his spelling.

The school was not a real school. The Irish were forbidden by law to have schools because the English were afraid if the Irish were educated, they would revolt against British rule. The children of wealthy Irish families were sent to England or France to be educated. But in Scotch Town, the only school was the secret school, called a hedge school, run by Master O'Grady in his kitchen. The school was secret because Squire Watson didn't know about it. As far as Devin was concerned, if the school was forbidden, then he shouldn't have to go, but his mother didn't agree. She said he would grow up to be a dunce if he didn't learn to read and write.

Devin said that he would rather grow up and be a

dunce than have to smell O'Grady's stinking crow breath. His mother made him go anyway.

As soon as school was finished, Devin and Katey would race out of Master O'Grady's house and run down the street as though they had just been freed from prison. But this particular morning, Katey had not come to school. Devin knew she had stayed home with a cold. When Devin had a cold, no one told him to stay at home or in bed. If he had a cough, his mother would boil two or three snails in barley water and then make him drink the water. But Katey's father was a doctor, and when Katey wasn't feeling well, her father made her stay in bed. He put leeches on her skin to draw out the bad blood. She had to stay in the house until she felt better.

Devin was rather vexed with Katey. It was early summer, and people shouldn't get sick in the summertime, when the days were long and warm. He took off his sweater. The potato fields were covered in white blossoms, and elder trees were in bloom. The keen fragrance of bog myrtle rose from the hillsides and ditches. Boys didn't get sick during the summer, he thought indignantly.

On the way home from school, he grabbed a tree branch and pulled himself up onto it. Then, putting his waist on the branch, he hung his head down from it, so that everything looked upside down.

The houses in the street were all upside down. The

thatched roofs were on the bottom and the stone foundations on top. Mrs. Flannagan, his mother's friend, carrying her basket and walking in the street, was upside down, so it looked as if she was walking on her head. An old wagon with wooden wheels creaked and squeaked by on the street. The horse and cart looked as if they were upside down.

"What is it you're doing?"

The voice came from behind Devin. He jumped down to see who it was and came face to face with Jimmy O'Brien.

Jimmy had been trying to be friends with Devin ever since he beat Paul Chandler. But since all Devin's efforts were spent trying to find food for the wolves, he didn't have much time to play with Jimmy O'Brien. Besides, sometimes Jimmy was still being friends with Paul Chandler.

"Not much," answered Devin.

"I can do that too," said Jimmy. "I've climbed right to the top of this tree."

"That's not much." Devin still had to catch some fish for the puppies. "I guess I better go now," he said.

Jimmy pulled a beautiful flute from beneath his shirt and began blowing it. The flute was nearly a foot long and made of ash wood, a golden-brown color. It was shiny and polished and waxed so that it gleamed in the sun.

"Hey," said Devin, "that's a wheen nice thing. Where'd you get it?"

"My father made it for me."

And Jimmy turned the flute. The sun caught it one more time, and Jimmy blew into it again. This time, the sound was soft, delicate, like the cooing of a dove.

Jimmy's father was always whittling things for him. Sometimes he whittled tops and painted them in bright colors, green and red and yellow. Sometimes he whittled pieces that fit together like puzzles to make shapes of things. Sometimes the shapes made a house, or a wheel, or a cart, or even a tree.

Devin's grandfather whittled shapes out of wood all the time too. But when Devin asked his Papli to whittle him a puzzle like Jimmy O'Brien's, his grandfather's puzzle didn't fit together the way Jimmy's did. And the tops his Papli whittled didn't spin either. And even though Papli whittled animal shapes — dogs, cows, birds — they were never as nice as those animal shapes that Jimmy's father made. Devin's grandfather's shapes always looked as if they'd been whittled by a monkey with five thumbs.

Devin's father didn't whittle at all. Devin once asked him to whittle a puzzle. His father's thin lips had turned downward, and he had said, "Whittlin'. Why, whittlin's for old men, lad. Whittlin'! I ain't got time to be whittlin', boy!"

Devin's fingers ached to hold the shiny, polished flute, to put his fingertips on the three holes along the top, and his heart ached to make that beautiful sound. "Will you let me see it?" he asked.

Jimmy went right on playing as though he didn't hear.

"Please?" said Devin.

Jimmy continued playing. The sounds rose high into the tree and floated from leaf to leaf as though the notes were splendidly colored butterflies, some green, some yellow with blue circles, some white.

"Jimmy. Please? Will you give me a look-see?"

Jimmy stopped playing. "My father said I wasn't to give it to nobody." He twirled the flute in his fingers, the gleaming ash wood catching the sun. To Devin, it looked as though the flute was made of gold.

Jimmy lifted it to his lips again and blew.

"Come on, Jimmy. Don't be so selfish."

Jimmy stopped playing again. "What'll you give me if I let you have a play?"

Devin scratched his ear for a moment, then reached deep into his trouser pocket. "You can look at my jack-knife."

"I've already had your jackknife. It's nothing."

Devin felt in the other pocket. He felt the soft fur of the rabbit's foot and the sharp claw. He pulled it out of his pocket and showed it to Jimmy. "How about this?"

Jimmy stopped playing. He looked at Devin's hand with a dismissive expression. He crinkled up his nose so that the freckles on it all bunched together. For a moment Jimmy looked as though he were trying to smell something. With the very tip-tips of his fingers, he reached out for the rabbit's foot. "Hmmm," he said in a bored tone, lifting it and looking at it briefly.

"It's good luck! It really is," Devin insisted.

Jimmy uncrinkled his nose and put the rabbit's foot back on Devin's palm. "You just have boring trinkets." And he put the flute back to his lips and played again.

"I do not have trinkets."

"You do so," Jimmy said between blows on the flute. "Do you want to hear something wheening funny?" And he made a sound on the flute like a hic-cough. "Imagine if O'Grady heard this!" said Jimmy, and he made several sounds through his flute. He made them higher, lower, then loud and explosive.

Devin was laughing. "Remember the time you were reading out loud and I started hiccoughing?"

The students had all been sitting in Master O'Grady's house. Everyone in the class heard, and they smothered their mouths with their hands so Master O'Grady couldn't see them laughing. Then Devin had hiccoughed again, and two other boys joined him. Master O'Grady's face wrinkled with anger, but he still didn't know who was making the sounds.

Then Master O'Grady had slammed his cane against

the floor. As he slammed his cane, his scarf got hooked in its handle and the scarf fell to the dirt floor. Master O'Grady bent down and picked it up, and Devin jumped up and secretly made an ugly face behind O'Grady's back. But he tripped over Katey's foot and fell squarely on top of Master O'Grady. Master O'Grady fell toward the bench and toppled it over, along with the four children sitting on it, including Katey. Half the class ended up in a heap on the floor. Master O'Grady hurt his back, and Katey's father had to keep putting leeches on it, and there had been no school for a month.

"What a lark that was!" Devin said happily.

Jimmy made more sounds on his flute, and they both laughed and laughed. And suddenly in their laughter it seemed as though the two boys were friends again.

"Come on. Give me a see of your flute."

"I would if you had something not half bad. Hey, listen to this," Jimmy said. And he blew another sound. "If O'Grady heard this, we wouldn't have school for a year."

Devin made sounds with just his mouth. They both laughed even harder. And then Devin decided that Jimmy was his friend again. "I can show you something that's not boring!" he said.

"What is it?"

"You have to swear not to tell anybody."

"I swear! What is it?"

"Cross your heart and hope to die if you tell a lie."

Jimmy's interest was really piqued now. Secrecy always meant that it was something special. "Cross my heart and hope to die if I tell a lie."

"And you promise you'll let me play your flute?"

Jimmy looked at his flute. "Depends on what it is you show me."

"Promise now, or I won't show you."

Jimmy scratched his head. "I promise."

"Wolf pups."

Jimmy grimaced, as though he hadn't really heard Devin. "What?"

"Wolf pups. Three of them."

"Their mother . . . if she finds us, she'll eat us up."

"They don't have a mother. Squire Watson killed her. Katey and me saw him do it. With a gun."

Jimmy passed the shiny wooden flute to Devin.

Devin lifted it to his lips and blew with delight. He stopped for a moment. "Katey and I have to get food for the wolves," he said. "You can help us."

Then, walking in the direction of Barne's Gap with Jimmy beside him, Devin piped happily.

12

When Jimmy returned to the front of his house after seeing the cubs, a small stone hit him in the shin. He knew immediately who had thrown the stone. This was the way Paul Chandler always got his attention. Jimmy had been eager, in the past, to play with Paul; now he no longer wanted to do so.

"Sly dog. Where is it you've been all afternoon?" Paul asked.

Jimmy shrugged. Devin had asked him to help get some food for the wolf pups. When Jimmy's mother cooked bacon with cabbages, the skin got all rubbery. Jimmy planned to ask his mother for the skin so he could take it to the young wolves tomorrow. "I'd better go in," he said. "My mother will be wanting to see me."

"What are you, some kind of baby, that you always have to be running to her?"

"No."

"Then come here. I want to show you something." Paul looked at Jimmy and smiled. "Just for a minute."

Paul came close and grabbed the flute that was sticking out of Jimmy's pocket.

"Hey! Give that back!"

But Paul ran to the back of the house. "You want it, come and get it!" Paul stopped and blew on the flute, and then as Jimmy approached he leaped out of the way, only to do the same thing again. Jimmy was slightly clumsy and didn't have a chance of catching Paul.

"I saw you leave with runt-face De-e-vin. Tell me what you did."

This news stunned Jimmy. He stopped chasing Paul and said, "We just walked. Tried to catch some mice. Give it back."

"This is a great fine flute, Jimmy."

"Hand it back. It's mine."

Paul dropped it to the ground.

"Hey! You'll scratch it." Jimmy shoved at Paul.

The two boys scuffled, but Paul remained unyielding as a sea cliff. When the scuffle was over, Jimmy was sitting on the ground, his head hanging. Paul stood with his booted foot on the flute.

"Tell me where you went with Devin, or I'll break it."

"We didn't go nowhere, I tell you. Now give me my flute, Paul. Please?" Jimmy tried to wriggle the flute out from beneath Paul's boot. "It's mine. My dad made it for me."

Paul rolled the flute back and forth under his boot.

"You're scratching it! My flute. My flute. Give me my flute, Paul." Jimmy was crying now, and he got on his hands and knees. "Please?"

"You want your flute? Tell me what you did." Paul's voice was hard, like a stone's edge. He bit his lower lip as he waited for Jimmy to answer him.

"I can't. I made a promise."

"A promise? Who'd you make a promise to? To De-e-vin?"

Jimmy didn't answer.

"Who'd you promise?" Paul rolled the flute harder so it made a crunching sound.

Jimmy knew now that the flute would no longer be the same. The stones had scratched and scraped it. Never again would he be able to hold the flute in the sun and watch the sun gleam in the polished wood. *Take care of it, me boy,* Jimmy's father had said when he handed it to Jimmy. *It took me a dreadful long time to be making it.*

But he had made a promise and he wouldn't tell. He remembered the way the wolf cubs had licked at his face and at his ears, and how they brought back a stick he threw to them. He remembered their wet, black noses and blue eyes.

The flute crunched harder against the rough gravel. "Tell me, Jimmy, what did you see?"

"I won't tell you. I won't! I won't!" And under Paul's big boot, the flute splintered.

Jimmy turned on him and said, crying, "You're nothing but a big stinking bully. I won't tell you what I saw with Devin this afternoon. You could break a thousand million flutes and I still wouldn't tell you."

❀13❀

*t*he next day was Saturday, and in the morning Devin had chores to do. First he had to milk Branwen and then he had to clean out Branwen's pen. This he did with a pitchfork and a wheelbarrow, and he had to carry out the manure to the garden, where it was used for fertilizer. And then he had to go down to the mill and bring back enough feed for Branwen for a week. And then he had to weed the garden. Weeding the garden was boring, and he hated it. He offset some of his boredom by eating the sweet green peas that had just begun to swell in the pods.

In the afternoon, finally, when all of his work was done, Devin waited for Jimmy in the tavern. It had felt good to play with Jimmy again, to laugh with him and to race along the road with him, to pitch stones, to see who could throw them the farthest, to pick up a stick and pretend to be sword-fighting. Devin had missed doing all of these things. He was glad that he and Jimmy were friends again. Jimmy really liked the pups too, and had promised to bring some food from his house.

Finally Jimmy arrived. Devin's mother stood by a side counter, where she was rolling out dough for kidney pies. "May the sun be shining on you, Jimmy," she greeted him. "What's been keeping you from calling on us this past while?"

Jimmy glanced at Devin and shrugged. "Not much."

"What is it you'll be carrying in your pack?" Devin's mother asked.

"Food for Bebo," Devin quickly answered for Jimmy.

Devin's mother set down her rolling pin and came close to where the two boys were standing. She wiped the flour off her hands. "What are the two of you scheming at?" she asked.

"Nothing," answered Devin.

"Don't think I haven't been noticing the strange way you're behaving, Mr. Smart Breeches. Sneaking out every chance you get. Picking up every morsel of meat you can put your hands on."

"It's for Bebo," Devin insisted.

"With all the food you've been carting off, Bebo would be roly-poly like an ale barrel. She couldn't be trotting about the way she does."

"Katey asked me to bring it," said Jimmy weakly.

"Now listen to me, the two of you," said Devin's mother. "Contrary to what you're thinking, I'm not a fool. And you'll not be leaving my front door until you tell me the truth about all these secret comings and goings." She crossed her arms in front of her.

Devin looked at his mother. She stood firmly planted between him and the door. The lines about her mouth were set in a deep and determined fashion. He couldn't tell her the truth about the wolves. His mother had a kind heart. She always managed to find scraps of food and the odd bit of cast-off clothing to give to the beggars and their children who passed through town looking for handouts, but she wouldn't understand about the wolves. She thought that wolves killed people, just as everybody else thought they did.

Devin stammered as his tongue tried to find words his mother would believe. "It's for . . . We found some . . ." He cleared his throat. "We found some pups." He wasn't really lying, as much as telling a half-truth. The wolves *were* like pups. "Some orphans out beyond the town."

"You're feeding stray dogs, while hungry people come begging at my door every day?" she asked.

"I just take table scraps," he said. "Nothing else. If we don't feed them, they'll die."

The lines around his mother's mouth softened. "Devin, you're kindhearted, but if they're strays, the townspeople will kill them."

Devin glanced at Jimmy, then looked back at his mother. "Can we go now?" he asked.

"How long do you plan on feeding them?" his mother asked.

Devin hadn't thought of how long he was going to have to continue getting food for the wolves. He knew that one day they would be able to hunt for themselves. Already, around the den that he and Katey had found for the pups, he had seen that the wolves chased mice and squirrels and sometimes caught and ate them, but he didn't know when they would be old enough to catch bigger prey. He shrugged his answer.

"How many pups are there?"

Devin swallowed. How many more questions would his mother ask? "Three," he said reluctantly.

"I'll start asking people here in the tavern if they know anyone that wants a dog."

"No," he answered quickly. "They're still afraid of people. Their mother was killed. Katey and I found her."

"Then you and Katey had better be finding them a home because they'll be shot as wild dogs." She returned to the counter where she was making her pies.

Devin and Jimmy scooted out of the tavern. Devin was so relieved to be free of his mother's questioning that he forgot his customary caution. He and Jimmy ran down the street as quickly as they could.

❧ 14 ❧

On Sunday morning Devin was anxious to go back out to the wolf pups, but his mother insisted that he go to church with her.

Because of the English laws, Catholics were not allowed to own land or to go to Catholic chapels. Before Devin was born, his grandfather had sworn an oath of faithfulness to the English church in order to keep his house, so Devin and his mother went to the English church. But Devin's mother had a string of Catholic rosary beads that her mother had given her. She kept them hidden under her bed, and sometimes when there was no one in the tavern, Devin had seen her take the beads and kneel in front of the hearth and pray. When she went to church on Sunday mornings, she hid the beads in her pocket.

Once Devin had asked her about them, and she had said, "Despite the laws that men make on earth, God in Heaven will know me for a Catholic woman."

Devin didn't understand the laws. Nor did he care about them right now.

Yesterday, when he and Jimmy had been with the wolves, Devin had thought he glimpsed Paul Chandler's pale head through the trees, but when Devin had run into the forest looking for Paul, there was no one there. Jimmy had assured Devin that Paul couldn't know about the pups. Devin, to be sure, wanted to move the wolves again, but Jimmy had to be home early. "I promise I'll help you move them tomorrow," Jimmy had said.

Katey was still sick, so Devin wasn't surprised when he walked into the stone church and saw she wasn't sitting beside her father.

Devin began to worry when he realized that Jimmy wasn't there either. Each time he heard the door to the church open, he twisted around in his seat to see if it was Jimmy who had come in late. The minister seemed to go on and on forever with his sermon. Devin fidgeted and twiddled his thumbs with impatience, until finally his mother whispered to him to be still.

It was then he noticed that Squire Watson wasn't in his private pew at the front of the church. Paul Chandler wasn't in the church either. Chandler didn't come to church often, but Devin couldn't help feeling that something was wrong. He fidgeted again. Despite the warmth of the sun outside, the stone building was cool inside. Devin began to shiver. He couldn't stop shivering as he sat on the wooden pew. His mother nudged his elbow, giving him a silent warning to be still, but Devin continued wriggling in his seat.

"Is it ants you've got in your breeches?" his mother whispered.

"Something's biting me," Devin whispered back.

"If you can't sit still, you'd better leave."

It was the only signal Devin needed.

Once he was outside the church, he began to run. He ran first to Jimmy's house. Inside he found Jimmy spitting and coughing, his face flushed as he sat close to the hearth fire. Jimmy hadn't come to church because he had caught a cold. He had a towel over his head and he was breathing the steam from a pot of hot water floating with spruce needles and mint leaves.

Seeing the spruce needles floating in the water reminded Devin of the branches with which he and Katey had hidden the wolves. From somewhere in the distance came the baying of Squire Watson's hounds.

Devin ran out of Jimmy's house without even stopping to close the door.

Mickey O'Rourke was out in his field hoeing potatoes. "Hey, laddie!" he shouted at Devin. "Where is it you'll be off to like your britches is on fire?" But Devin didn't answer.

As he reached the river, he was in such a hurry that he was going to plunge straight through without taking his shoes off. But a stone flew and hit him in the shin. Devin stopped running.

Paul Chandler appeared from behind a tree. "Well, if it isn't De-e-vin! What are you dong, De-e-vin? Looking for your wolves? I told Squire Watson about them. We came and found them this morning."

Devin wouldn't believe what Paul Chandler told him. Paul dropped coins from one hand to another, but the jingle of money sounded as though it were coming from far away. Paul's voice continued, but it too seemed to be coming from some distant place. "He even paid me. Thought you were smart, didn't you? Scouring them away. Bringing them food, and taking boxing lessons from that ape Costello. Thought you could beat me up. You're still nothing but a stupid runt. Shrimpy De-e-vin." Laughing, Paul ran off into the forest.

Screaming, Devin charged into the river and ran across, thrashing the water up around him in a great spray. As he ran, he prayed. "Please, God," he said. "Don't let what Paul said be true. Make it just a joke. Don't let anything be wrong with the puppies." But as he ran, there was a sickening feeling in his stomach, as though some rotting thing were lying there.

As he came to the tree that had been split by lightning, his heart flew into his throat. He thought that the branches in front hadn't been moved at all. Paul had just been lying. Everything was the same. Everything was all right. Devin ran ahead even more quickly.

But then he stopped. The branches *had* been moved back. And there on the ground . . . blood!

But Devin wouldn't believe it. He screamed out the names of the puppies. "Sdhoirm! Dun! Beg!" He whistled. And he screamed out their names again. But no puppies came. He raced through the forest and looked under bushes, yelling their names. But he didn't find the puppies anywhere. Finally he came back to the den. And there it was again. Blood! Squire Watson had shot them just as he had shot their mother. And it was Devin's fault. He should have moved the puppies yesterday when he wanted to. It was his fault.

Devin's chest hurt as though someone wearing heavy boots had repeatedly kicked him. Crying, he crawled into the den where the wolf cubs had curled up and slept. He pulled his knees against his face and clasped his arms around his legs, trying to stop the hurt, but it wouldn't go away. The cave was filled with the wolf smell of memory, and Devin remembered the night he had brought them here, the way the small wolves had cocked their heads to one side, one ear up, one ear down, the way their soft pink tongues licked at his face, his palms, and he cried harder.

❀ 15 ❀

espairing grief overwhelmed Devin, drew him into sleep. His hands relaxed around his ankles. His breathing grew deep and regular, and soon, in his dreams, he was playing beside a river. He was throwing a stick, and the three wolf puppies were around him, leaping and barking. He threw a stick to Sdhoirm, and Sdhoirm leaped up and caught it in midair and then brought it back to him.

As Devin dreamed, a mist was gathering on top of the mountains, rolling down them until they were obscured. The mist reached out with silent, secret fingers and touched one blade of grass and then another. It crept up the tree trunks and along the branches, and then it billowed to the ground. An ant that was carrying a seed back to its nest disappeared, the anthill disappeared, and more trees were swept up in the green-gray waves.

The mist came closer to where Devin slept. Stone by stone, it crept, and as it came closer, so too did an animal. An animal padding on silent paws. Four paws with clover-shaped pads and sharp claws. The animal sniffed its way, following its own scent because all the landmarks, the fallen trees, the stones, the hills, all were swept invisible in the mist that had fallen from the mountains.

The animal came close to the tree split by lightning, and it picked up Devin's fresh scent. It stopped and sniffed at a rock, and then at the base of the tree where the ground fell away, and then at a pile of rotting leaves, for the animal discovered other scents too. Strange scents, something that smelled like the human smell of Devin, but not the same, and there were other smells as well.

And as the animal came close, Devin slept. He no longer sat, but was lying down on the bed of leaves and branches that he and Katey had made for the pups. He lay on his side with his left hand stretched out. The mist lay over the hills now, and the entrance to the cave where Devin slept was covered with a haze. A finger of fog reached into the cave, but there the warmth from Devin's body dissipated it. Then a gust of breeze came and lifted the mist, and it billowed and rose and continued on its silent, secret way, passing over Devin.

But the silent paws of the animal came closer. It sniffed everywhere as it approached, for everywhere was the strange human scent. And just at the entrance of the cave, the animal stopped, for it came to a pool of blood. It didn't understand the blood smell. The animal sniffed again and whined, and then came closer to Devin and sniffed at the soles of his shoes.

Devin heard the animal whining, but he was lost in his dream, and his ears caught the sound of the whine and carried it into his dream. In his dream he was running across a meadow. He was running with Katey and Bebo and Sdhoirm. There were yellow gorse flowers everywhere in the field. And Devin carried a stick, and as he ran he threw the stick, and Sdhoirm, who was no longer a puppy but a full-grown wolf, ran ahead and leapt up and caught the stick in midair and brought it back to him. Devin took the stick from Sdhoirm's mouth, and Sdhoirm began to whimper and whine and lick his hand because he wanted Devin to throw the stick again.

And now the animal in the cave whimpered and whined and licked at Devin's hand. It touched its cold, wet nose against Devin's palm, and then it began to lick at his palm.

Devin shifted in his sleep and drew his hand back,

but the animal followed the hand and continued to whine. And Devin's dream ended, and he took a deep breath, but still he felt something licking at his hand, and he opened his eyes and saw a large, gray-black animal. And Devin drew back, for it was a wolf.

But it was a small wolf, a puppy; a large puppy, but still a puppy. But it wasn't just any puppy, it was Sdhoirm, and it wasn't a dream anymore. Sdhoirm was here, licking at his face. Devin threw his arms around him and lifted and hugged him. He let the wolf lick his ears and his face and his neck.

Devin realized that Sdhoirm must have escaped from the den again and had been gone when Squire Watson came.

Devin had no choice now but to take Sdhoirm home with him. He picked the wolf up and carried him across the river. It had begun to rain, and rain dripped in Devin's collar and from his eyebrows into his eyes. The wolf was big and gangly and his claws scraped against Devin's stomach, so Devin put him down. Sdhoirm followed.

Devin took no chances. When he came close to town, he took off his sweater and covered Sdhoirm up, so only his tail showed. Uncomfortable and heavy as the wolf was, Devin carried him in behind the houses to his parents' stable. Rain was falling hard now, without any sign of letting up, and Devin met no one. The door of the stable was closed, which meant Branwen had been brought home from the pasture.

The wooden door of the stable squeaked horrendously and accusingly when Devin opened it. It seemed to shout, *Devin is bringing a wolf into this stable! Wolf! Wolf!* Devin hid inside, listening for approaching footsteps. But there were none. There was only the steady, muffling sound of rain pattering on the thatch and on the muddy ground outside.

He couldn't see Branwen at first, for his eyes were unaccustomed to the dimness, but the warm cow smell of her enveloped him in the stable. She mooed her quiet, affectionate welcome. Then he saw her staring at him, her hairy ears turned in his direction.

Devin uncovered the wolf. Sdhoirm jumped to the floor and began sniffing around at the straw. He sniffed at the straw behind the cow, then at the splayed hooves of her back feet. He sniffed his way to her front and stood on his hind legs to look into the manger. Branwen bent down to look at him, and Sdhoirm, in some way, seemed to sense her gentleness. He licked her wet nose.

"See, Branwen?" said Devin. "He's your friend."

Branwen looked at the wolf for a moment, then licked him. But her tongue nearly flattened Sdhoirm against the manger, so he yelped as though he were being skinned alive. Devin tried to come to the pup's defense, but as Devin bent down, Branwen gave him a quick lick to the side of the face.

"Branwen!" Devin yelled.

She turned her head from him, the hurt obvious in her eyes. Devin wrapped his arms around her neck, rubbed behind her ears, and scratched her forehead. "Your tongue is too rough!"

Branwen continued looking away.

"I love you," Devin said. "Don't sulk, please."

Branwen turned her hairy ears toward Devin.

"You have to be gentle with your tongue," he told her. "Sdhoirm is just a puppy. He's a wolf, but just a pup." Devin picked him up and held him for Branwen to sniff.

Sdhoirm wriggled at first, wildly frightened. But with Devin's petting and kind words, he quieted. When Branwen put her head down to Sdhoirm again, he licked her. Branwen kept her head close and Sdhoirm licked her for a long, long time, rhythmically, regularly, instinctively.

An enormous protective feeling came over Devin. He pulled the wolf cub close. Sdhoirm had no way of knowing what had happened to his family. The day his mother was killed, he must have waited for her to come back, must have squealed and whimpered and cried and howled. Today he must have smelled the pools of blood around the den where his sisters had been killed, and not understood what they meant. What could Devin, a boy, do with this wolf to make him understand Squire Watson's hounds and guns? Devin pulled Sdhoirm closer against his heart. The stable, warmed with Branwen's soft breath, was a shelter. He would keep the wolf here.

But Sdhoirm wriggled free and jumped into the manger, where he began to lick at his paws, for they were covered with burrs and bits of twig from his wanderings. He turned about on the hay three or four times and lay down and fell asleep immediately. In sleep, he whimpered.

Branwen nudged Sdhoirm gently with her nose and mooed softly in her throat. Devin put his arms around her neck and laid his head against hers. "You have to help me," he said. "We have to protect him." Branwen mooed softly again, as though she understood.

❧ 16 ❧

although it was summer, Devin, Katey, and Jimmy were not outside a great deal. Instead they spent almost all of their time in the stable, playing catch with each other and Sdhoirm. Often they simply sat and talked or told stories as they petted and stroked Sdhoirm and Bebo.

Whenever Devin spoke, Sdhoirm perked up his ears as though he understood every word. When Devin picked up the ball, Sdhoirm's intelligent, playful eyes seemed to twinkle mischievously. The young wolf loved to play.

But sometimes Sdhoirm would sit by the door and whine and howl softly.

"You can't go out there," Devin would say. "They'll shoot you!"

One day Katey, Devin, and Jimmy were just heading out the door of the tavern. Devin's mother, who was standing beside the butter churn, frowned at them and asked, "What is it that the three of you will always be finding to do in that stable?"

Devin and Katey looked at each other. Jimmy looked at the floor.

"We play," Katey said.

"With the weather being so nice and summery, surely the three of you can be outside instead of inside like chickens in a coop."

"We're not in a coop," Devin protested.

"I don't want you in there today, with the sun shining so splendidly. Soon it'll be turning to fall with the rain and cold. There'll be time enough to be indoors then."

"But —"

"And I won't be taking any of your back talk neither! Now, mind what I said."

Devin, Katey, and Jimmy went out the door of the tavern and down the street. Then they snuck back to the stable.

Devin had rubbed the hinges with bacon grease, and the children entered in absolute quiet. He had even tacked down the noisy horseshoe firmly with a hammer so it didn't bang anymore. Today he had a special plan.

Sdhoirm leaped up at Devin when he saw him, and whined and licked at his face. Devin buried his nose in the wolf's fur.

The problem with keeping Sdhoirm in the stable was that he had started howling. He didn't howl quite like a wolf yet, but sometimes . . . Devin was afraid that soon Sdhoirm would begin to sound exactly like a wolf. If he and Katey and Jimmy were in the stable, then Sdhoirm didn't howl, and when Branwen was with him at night, he didn't howl either. But during the day Branwen went out to the pasture. They couldn't continue keeping the wolf inside.

Devin had decided that if he clipped Sdhoirm's hair, the way the farmers clipped the sheep for wool, then he would look like a dog. He could tell his mother that he had found a stray dog. He would be able to take Sdhoirm for walks, and at night Sdhoirm could sleep in the tavern. No one would know the difference.

The previous night, when Devin had visited Mickey O'Rourke with his grandfather, he had secreted the clipping shears from the farmer's stable. Mr. O'Rourke wouldn't look for them again this year, since the sheep were always clipped in the spring. Devin would put back the shears the next time he visited with his grandfather. For the present he had hidden them under the hay in Branwen's manger.

Devin pulled them from their hiding place. They were long, scissor-looking things, made for a man's hands, and Devin felt awkward with them. As he lifted them, he tried to remember what the moon had been like the night before. He couldn't remember, but since Sdhoirm was a wolf, maybe the moon didn't matter.

Katey looked at the clippers and said, "You can't cut his hair!"

Sdhoirm looked at the shears, whined, then lowered his head and slunk to the back of the stable, where he flopped down.

"Come here, boy," Devin said. "It won't hurt. After, we'll be able to take you out like Bebo."

Bebo, who heard her name mentioned, came running, but when she saw the clippers, she gave several sharp yaps and scurried back to where Sdhoirm lay.

Katey stood with her heels together and pointed her finger at Devin. "Sheep look ridiculous when they're clipped. And Sdhoirm will look ridiculous if he's clipped."

Sdhoirm whined; Bebo yapped nervously.

Devin remained convinced that he was doing the right thing. "Come here, pup!" he called Sdhoirm.

The wolf, sensing something unusual, slunk over to Devin. The boy stroked him. Devin didn't want to frighten Sdhoirm, so he let him smell the clippers. Then he opened and closed them so that Sdhoirm could hear what they sounded like.

Sdhoirm flattened his ears against the sound. The *crunch, crunch* sound of the opening and closing shears frightened him.

"It's all right. There's nothing to be afraid of. It

won't hurt." He patted and stroked Sdhoirm, reassuring him. Jimmy petted him too. Sdhoirm's ears were flat against his head and his shoulders were hunched up, but he wagged his tail slowly.

Devin slid the shears through the thick ruff of the wolf's shoulders. He was going to clip —

"Devin!" The stable door opened and there stood his mother.

Devin dropped the clippers.

Sdhoirm hunched his shoulders and growled at the intruder.

"Devin! What in the name — Get away from that wolf!"

"He won't hurt anybody, he's tame. He's just little."

"'Tis a wolf!"

"But he's tame, Mother," and Devin bent down close to Sdhoirm's head.

In a moment Devin's mother could see that the wolf was not dangerous to her son. With his blue eyes, erect ears, and cocked head, the animal wore a curious expression as if to say, *What are you doing here?* She saw how Devin petted and stroked him without fear. But the fact remained. "You'll be having to take him back to where you found him."

"But Squire Watson will shoot him."

"What will people be saying when they find out 'tis a wolf we're keeping?"

"They won't know!"

"You can't be keeping a wolf in a stable. 'Tis a wild thing."

"Sdhoirm's not wild!" Devin bent down close again. Sdhoirm licked him and whimpered.

"'Tis not here he belongs!" Devin's mother said.

"But where does he belong?" Devin asked. "Out in the forest, people shoot them. They get money for killing them. They say they kill sheep and people! But Sdhoirm doesn't kill people. He didn't kill me. And his mother didn't kill me. He's good and gentle!" Devin argued. "If we clip him, no one will even know he's a wolf."

"Squire Watson killed his mother and his two sisters," Katey said.

Devin's mother walked over to Devin, Katey, and Jimmy. "You could be clipping all his hair off and he'd still be looking like a wolf," she said gently.

"No, he won't. No one will be able to tell the difference. His eyes are still blue like Bebo's one eye," said Katey. "Wolves have yellow eyes. Everybody knows that."

"Kittens' eyes change. His will too. Look at him. Look at Bebo! Everybody can be seeing the difference. You can't keep a wolf hidden."

"You keep your rosary hidden," Devin snapped. "And so does Katey's mother."

"'Tis different!" Devin's mother replied. "A rosary is for praying with to the good Lord."

"God made wolves just as he made me and you! You always say to treat God's creatures with kindness, but you won't be kind to Sdhoirm."

"I'm trying to be kind. At least in the forest he'll have a chance."

"He's too young. Can't you see he's too young?" Devin persisted.

"Please, Mrs. O'Hara," said Jimmy.

"Devin's father will be fit to murder a saint if he finds out," answered Devin's mother.

"He doesn't have to know," pleaded Devin. "He never comes in here."

Devin's mother sighed. "You can't be letting anybody see him. Clip him if you like, but he'll still look like a wolf. You'll have to be making sure he can look after himself when you set him free, and it's not by feeding him table scraps that he'll learn to do that. You'll have to take him into the forest at night and teach him to hunt."

Devin, Katey, and Jimmy all cheered as they hugged Sdhoirm. Even Bebo sensed the joy and yapped with excitement.

"Don't be so happy, all of you," warned Devin's mother. "You're just putting off what has to be."

17

Devin decided against clipping Sdhoirm. When his mother opened the stable door to leave, the light shining in on the wolf's eyes turned them to a peculiar color, more green than blue. In that moment Devin saw for himself that the pup's eyes would turn yellow. All the clipping in the world would not be able to hide the fact that Sdhoirm was a wolf and not a dog.

Deep in his heart, Devin knew that his mother was right. One day he would have to let Sdhoirm go. When the time came, Sdhoirm would need his fur to keep warm. The next day Devin sadly returned the clippers to Mickey O'Rourke.

Devin didn't want to wake his father when he left in the night to take Sdhoirm hunting, so he began sleeping in the stable. He told his father he didn't like to sleep with all the strangers in the tavern.

"It's a fine thing," Devin's father said, "my boy sleeping in the stable."

Devin's mother interceded. "Jesus was born in a stable," she said. "If it was a good enough place for our Lord, it's a good enough place for a boy."

Devin's father didn't question him again.

After dark Devin took Sdhoirm with him out into the night. The wolf was already catching mice and rats in the stable, so Devin assumed that Sdhoirm would learn to catch them easily in the forest. He was right. The wolf's keen nose scented out the small rodents, and before Devin and Sdhoirm returned home, the wolf had caught over a dozen of the scurrying creatures.

Devin and Sdhoirm went out night after night. The wolf enjoyed these outings tremendously, and when Devin opened the stable door after dark, Sdhoirm seemed to fly at Devin with excitement, nearly knocking him off his feet.

Although Sdhoirm was tamed, instinct surfaced in him. He began chasing rabbits.

Devin watched him with a mixture of joy and regret. On one hand, Devin was happy that Sdhoirm's hunting skills were developing. But secretly he was glad that the wolf was still too slow to catch the speedy rodents. As long as Sdhoirm was clumsy, Devin could continue to tell his mother that the wolf was too young to let go.

Devin no longer went to the blacksmith shop to box with Costello. Devin had beaten Paul Chandler, yet Paul Chandler had taken revenge. Devin felt an overwhelming sadness each time he thought of Dun and Beg.

Katey was unable to go with Devin at night. Sometimes Jimmy could sneak away after dark, but mostly it was Devin alone who took Sdhoirm hunting.

Over the summer Devin's mother helped him keep his secret. She gathered whatever leftovers she could from the tavern and gave them to Devin. But she did so more and more reluctantly.

Each day a greater number of beggars came to her door, many of them near starvation because they'd been chased off their land by the English.

"Devin," she said to him quietly one day after Sdhoirm had been in the stable about a month. "You have to let Sdhoirm go now. People are going hungry in this country."

"Please, not yet!" Devin pleaded. "He's not big enough."

"We can't keep feeding him much longer," his mother replied.

Devin took Sdhoirm to the Glenelly River. At first

the wolf was perplexed and didn't realize he was supposed to catch fish. Devin shone a light on the water, and using a net he caught a couple of trout and dumped them wriggling on the ground. Sdhoirm gulped them down.

Now the wolf sensed what he was supposed to do. He leaped into the river, and as Devin shone the light on the water, Sdhoirm snatched up trout after trout in his jaws, devouring them in a single swallow.

By the time fall came, Sdhoirm had grown, so that he was bigger than Bebo. He had become a magnificent animal, dark gray with a white ruff and yellow eyes that glowed in the dim light of the stable. Devin, too, had grown. His mother had to sew him two new pairs of breeches because his old ones were too small for him and cut tightly into his thighs above his knees.

The purple flowers of the thistle withered to gray, like the beards of old men in the chill fall air.

Devin's mother told him that he couldn't take any more food from the tavern. "If you keep feeding Sdhoirm, he'll never be learning to look after himself."

With hunger as a teacher, the wolf caught his first rabbit, and then a badger.

The night Sdhoirm killed the badger, he lifted his head to the sky and howled.

"Sssh." Devin wrapped his arms around the wolf's neck. "If you howl, Squire Watson will find you."

But the wolf didn't seem to understand. He raised his voice again in a lonely, haunting sound that brought tears to Devin's eyes. Devin knew he would have to let Sdhoirm go.

The next day, in the tavern, Devin listened with anxiety to the conversations of the patrons sitting around a table.

"I heard a wolf howl last night!" one man said.

"Aye, I did too," said a second man.

"I thought Squire Watson killed the last of them devils."

"No one can kill all the wolves," said the second man.

The first snow dusted the ground and the withering blossoms of flowers in a coating of white. The conversation in the tavern was animated the next day.

"I saw wolf tracks in the snow in Barne's Gap," said a traveler.

"Aye," answered one of the townsmen. "I've heard a wolf howling close by."

"These tracks were big," answered the traveler. "The size of a man's palm."

"Wolves don't grow that big," protested Devin.

"What do you know of wolves, lad?" rebuked the traveler. "I saw them tracks meself. Leading straight here to town, they were. That devil will be eating you, my lad, if you're not careful."

"Wolves don't eat people," insisted Devin. "They —"

"Devin," his mother interrupted. "Come and help me fill the ale jug."

That night Devin's mother came into the stable. She was wrapped in a shawl to ward off the chill.

The moment Devin saw her, he knew why she'd come, and he began to plead with her.

"We can't send Sdhoirm out now. It's winter," he said.

"Look at the fur on him, my son. He's a wild thing. You've taught him to hunt. He'll be fine."

"But Squire Watson will kill him when he finds him."

"They'll kill him when they find him here." His mother's voice was kind but unyielding as she continued. "At least in the wild he'll have a chance to survive. He can go somewhere. Into the mountains where Squire Watson won't be hunting. Where he'll be with his own kind."

"There aren't any other wolves left. Squire Watson said he wouldn't rest as long as there was one alive."

"Everybody says that. Nobody means it, surely!"

"But he meant it. I heard him."

"Nobody can be killing all the wolves. 'Tis exaggerating, they are."

"But they can. I haven't heard any wolves howl anywhere."

"Well, I head him howling the other day. It was low

enough I could tell your father it was just one of the town dogs. But Sdhoirm's almost full-grown now. One day, he'll be letting out a grown wolf's howl, and every man in town will be here. With pitchforks, knives, sticks, guns. How long do you think he'll live then? Where could he be hiding in here?" His mother moved her arm in the direction of the back wall. "He'd be trapped and dead in the wink of an eye. In the mountains he'd have a fair chance to be running away. But there's no place for him to run here."

Devin was crying quietly now, for he knew his mother was right. There was nothing for him to do but to take Sdhoirm and let him go.

❧18❧

*T*he night sky was a turmoil of clouds. Devin and Sdhoirm walked in Barne's Gap, in the direction of the mountains. It took a long time to reach the Glenelly River because Devin walked very slowly.

After they had crossed the river, Devin stopped walking and knelt beside Sdhoirm. As he did so, he saw a shape in the clouds. To Devin it looked like the head of the wolf he had seen that day in the mist by Barne's Gap. And he thought that perhaps it was Sdhoirm's mother who had gone to heaven and was looking down, watching over him, making certain that Sdhoirm would be all right.

Devin held Sdhoirm's head and pointed to the clouds. "Look there," he said. "See the wolf?"

Sdhoirm whined and licked his lips, but he was too excited to look in any one direction. He thought he was coming out to go hunting again. He didn't like being in the stable all day. He was free again, free to listen to the outdoor sounds, to the hooting of an owl or the wind in the pines. Free to smell again those smells that he knew, the foresty pine smell and the smell of the moon. He lifted his dark head and howled.

Devin buried his face in the wolf's thick ruff. How many hours he had spent with Sdhoirm, playing with him, petting him, teaching him to catch a ball in his mouth, to bring back a stick, to sit, and to stay in one place while Devin walked around the stable.

Sdhoirm rested his head on Devin's shoulder, then touched his cold, wet nose against Devin's neck and whined as though he knew what Devin was thinking. Sdhoirm licked at the tears that trickled down Devin's cheek. Devin's heart felt as though it would break in two.

He told himself what his mother had told him: A wolf's howl would bring every man in Scotch Town running to the stable. Devin told himself that Sdhoirm would run up into the mountains where he could live, and find another wolf. He told himself that Sdhoirm would find a cave and be safe there. But even though he said these things in his mind, his heart didn't believe them.

At that moment the moon came out from behind the clouds. It was a crescent moon. Devin's mother always said that if the moon looked as though you could hang your hat on it, it was a good luck sign. In the moonlight the dark head of the wolf silvered. The ground was covered with frost.

"Sit," Devin said.

Sdhoirm sat.

"Stay," Devin said. Devin began to walk away, but Sdhoirm stood and whimpered. "Stay!" Devin ordered.

Sdhoirm whimpered, louder this time.

"You can't come back!" Devin cried. "You have to go there," Devin pointed, "up to the mountains. You'll be safe there. You'll find more wolves."

But Sdhoirm took a couple of steps toward him.

"No," Devin cried. "That way!"

Sdhoirm looked in the direction that the boy pointed, then walked to Devin.

Devin knelt down and took Sdhoirm's head in his hands again. He couldn't stop crying. "You can't come home with me. You have to go away."

The wolf whined, then raised his paw to rest it on Devin's shoulder, as though he understood what the boy wanted. Devin sobbed, his shoulders shaking against the wolf.

A cloud covered the moon. The mountains and the river and trees were in total darkness, indistinguishable from each other.

The wolf whined again. Devin remembered his rabbit's foot and took it from his pocket. He removed his shoelace, attached it to the good luck charm, then tied it about the wolf's neck. "This will protect you," he said. The crescent moon appeared again, like a silver claw in the darkness.

Sdhoirm whimpered. Then he stood and began to trot in the direction of the mountains. A few dozen feet away, he stopped. Moon-silvered, he turned toward Devin.

"Go!" the boy shouted. "Run! As far as you can!" He began to walk away, and the wolf whined. Devin continued walking. He heard the lonely howl behind him, as though Sdhoirm was asking him to stay. Devin began to run and did not stop until he reached home. He knew if he turned around, even for a moment, his heart would surely break.

Late that night, as he lay in bed, he heard Sdhoirm howl from far away. "Harrrroooooo, harrrrrroooo." It was the loneliest, saddest sound that he had ever heard. It seemed to him that Sdhoirm was calling to his mother, to his sisters, and to every wolf that had ever been killed in Ireland. Devin buried his face in his pillow and wept.

❧ 19 ❧

*t*hree years passed after Devin sent Sdhoirm off into the mountains. Eventually he carried his bed back into the tavern. He took a spurt and grew, so that he was taller than his mother.

Scotch Town was a small town. Devin's mother eventually told someone that her son had kept a wolf in the stable, and the news spread about town. For a while Devin was ridiculed, but then people forgot about the wolf and went on with the business of their lives — digging potatoes, planting oats, raising sheep.

Sometimes at night, in the distance, Devin would hear the woeful, lonely howling of a wolf, so faint it almost sounded like an echo.

And then stories started circulating about a great, huge wolf in the mountains. These stories were told by travelers who came to the Black Boar Tavern, and

Devin would listen to them as he served up the pitchers of ale.

"He's as big as a bull! And black as hell! I seen him with me own eyes," one traveler said.

"The bottom of your ale cup. That's all you was seein'," someone else shouted.

"That black devil killed a dozen sheep at one time, the other side of the river," the traveler said.

"Ain't a wolf alive what'll kill a dozen sheep at one time," said the other man at the table.

"A dozen sheep, I tell you. I took a shot at him. The bullet went into him. I seen it with these eyes. But he's half devil, that one. Kept right on running."

Devin rarely saw Paul Chandler. The bully worked full days in the butcher shop along with his father.

"You can't be trusting either of them," Devin's mother always said. "Always weighing the scales down with their fingers. Crooked as a crab's toe, the both of them."

The owner of the blacksmith shop died, and Thomas Costello married his widow. In addition to the blacksmith's four children, Thomas Costello now had two babies of his own. Devin hardly saw Thomas anymore. Devin was nearly thirteen, and soon he would be helping his father in the quarry, cutting out stone to build houses.

One day, as Devin and Katey were walking on the other side of the Glenelly River, they heard shots and the barking and baying of dogs. On a distant hill, Devin saw something running, a black blur. Immediately he knew what it was. He shouted, "Sdhoirm! Sdhoirm!" and the black blur lifted its head.

Sdhoirm seemed to sniff the wind, he howled, and then he was gone again. Devin and Katey ran after him, but he had disappeared in the hills.

Periodically Devin would get a glimpse of Sdhoirm on some distant hill. Once Devin saw him nearby, and Sdhoirm whined and approached him. Devin had never seen such a splendid animal. The wolf's head was wide and broad and majestic as the mountains themselves. Then the baying of dogs sounded and Sdhoirm was off again.

The stories about Sdhoirm grew. "I tell you, I wouldn't be walking the hills as long as it's alive."

"I seen him. And his eyes is red as the fires of hell," said a man with a face scarred with pimples and pox. The man set his wooden ale cup heavily on the table.

"He doesn't have red eyes," Devin said angrily. "They're yellow."

"Are you calling me a liar?" said the scar-faced man. Long shadows from a candle darkened his face. To Devin the man looked a thousand times more dangerous than any animal.

"Leave him be," said another man with a black moustache. "He's just a silly sheephead. He tried to raise up a wolf in his mother's own stable."

"Raise a wolf? Someone ought to shoot him. Raising a wolf. Feeding it, when there's people in this land what's starving to death."

"Ain't no more wolves left in Ireland. This here wolf is the last one," said someone else.

"Well, I seen him. His eyes was red, I tell you. Red like this here handkerchief."

Devin wondered why adults always believed other adults and not children, even when it was the adults who were lying and the children who were telling the truth.

The stories about Sdhoirm became more terrifying with each telling. "They put out poison bait for that devil. But he ate it and survived."

"He attacked a coach traveling up through the Gortin Forest. Killed the driver. Leapt out of a tree at him."

"That was highwaymen. Wolves can't be climbing trees."

"It was the wolf. They saw wolf marks on the path. The footman told me."

"Sdhoirm wouldn't kill anybody," Devin said.

Devin's father replied to the other men in the tavern, "Look at my son. Silly enough, he was, to raise that devil in his own parents' stable."

And so Devin stopped talking about Sdhoirm. Deep in his heart, he knew that Sdhoirm didn't do any of those things. Often in the evenings, he would walk out to Barne's Gap. Sometimes he would walk alone, and sometimes he would walk with Katey and Bebo.

In the tavern the stories about Sdhoirm continued. Now they were told in hushed, frightened voices, as though the speakers thought the wolf would come through the very walls of the tavern like some evil specter.

"He's a devil wolf. A red-eyed demon!"

"There's a triple bounty on him now. Fifty shillings for his hide."

"There ain't nothing what can catch that creature. Not guns. Not poison. Not traps. Not dogs."

It was early spring in 1786 and a wild March wind blew off the ocean. Devin was walking along Barne's Gap, and far, far in the distance, he heard something. He stopped and listened for a moment, and he decided that the sounds were just the wind, for the wind coming through the trees sometimes sounded like an animal. He listened again. The sound was the baying of hounds. Devin heard shots in the distance.

Each time over the past years that Devin had heard shots, he thought of Sdhoirm. But at night in the tavern, his mother would reassure him that Sdhoirm had always managed to escape. Devin was certain Sdhoirm would escape again.

In the mountains Devin saw the mist gathering. He turned and headed for home. Although he no longer thought of himself as a boy, he still believed in the dullahan coach and the headless phantoms.

Late that night Devin was wakened by something. At first he wasn't even certain what had woken him, or even that he was awake. He heard sounds. There was a great thrashing of branches against the window, but there was another sound. A door slammed in the wind, and slammed again, and slammed once more. But there was something else in the wind. It was the constant and persistent mooing of a cow, and Devin shook himself awake. He wasn't dreaming. It was Branwen. But why was Branwen making such a noise in the middle of the night?

The cold March air gave Devin goose pimples as he stepped from the warmth of his bed. He pulled on his breeches and buttoned his shirt and yanked a sweater over his head.

Outside the wind was howling like a madman. The tree beside the house was bent nearly to the ground. A storm was near and dark black clouds were being pushed across the sky. The moon appeared, but just for a moment, and was swept away again behind the dark, tumultuous clouds. And then Branwen mooed again.

Perhaps she was afraid of the storm. Devin pulled on his socks and shoes as quietly as he could.

The house was black as a pit. Devin couldn't see anything. He looked where he knew the fire was.

Every night his mother covered the living, burning coals in ashes to keep them hot for the next morning's use.

Tonight even the fire seemed pitch black. He felt his way across the dirt floor. His mother and father were sleeping on the other side, close to the wall. Devin couldn't see his grandfather, but he heard him snoring in his big oak chair close to the hearth. Devin could see nothing. He judged where he was in the room by the sound of his grandfather's snores.

When they were smaller, he and Katey had played a game. One would close his or her eyes very tight, and the other would call. The first person would try and find the second, strictly by his or her voice. Devin felt as though he was doing that now, except in reverse. He was moving away from his grandfather's snores. Then from the stable he heard Branwen mooing again.

Devin knew he was getting close to the door, and he reached out with his fingers in the darkness, groping, yet touching nothing. His mind was on the door when he tripped and crashed to the floor, making enough noise to wake the dead. But he was lucky, for at that moment a great crack of thunder shook the air. It shook the very walls of the house. At the same time, the entire tavern lit up with a brilliance that was brighter than daylight, and Devin saw that he had tripped on a stool someone had left sticking out from under a table.

Devin lifted himself from the floor. His grandfather moaned in his sleep, then resumed snoring. Devin heard his mother turn and sigh, and then she, too, continued sleeping.

Devin opened the door to the tavern ever so slowly, but the wind grabbed it and slammed it open. The gust made the curtains fly.

Devin pulled the door shut behind him as quickly as he could. The wind took away his breath.

Outside, total darkness swallowed him. There were no stars, no moon, only the fierce and violent wind. Devin felt his way along the edge of the house; tree branches slapped at his face. Above the howl of the wind, he heard the steady slam, slam of the stable door, and the mooing of Branwen. The darkness was a tangle of black wind.

Devin reached the stable and lightning flashed again, awesome and frightening in its brilliance, as though the whole world was caught in a white fire. And there on the ground in front of him, he saw a red pool of blood! Then the lightning faded. Thunder struck through the darkness like a hammer. Devin felt the earth rumble. He felt the terrible chill of the night, but more, he felt the chill of fear. Was it really blood he had seen? Was it just the lightning playing tricks with his eyes?

In the pure darkness, he knelt down and groped the ground with his fingers. He touched only stones, first one ragged shape after another, and then he touched the congealed, cold liquid.

Devin had never been so afraid in his life. His heart, his stomach, his lungs. All of them were at the back of his throat. The muscles of his eyes throbbed as he tried to see in the unyielding blackness. The sky lit again. Devin lifted his fingers: they were bloodstained.

"Branwen!" Devin called. What if it wasn't Branwen, but a ghost making a sound like Branwen? What if it was a dullahan that had dumped the blood here? What if it was a highwayman or robber who had been shot and was hiding in the stable with his big knife, ready to chop off Devin's head?

Devin was afraid to step into the stable, but he was afraid to go back into the house now, for it sounded as though something was behind him. He heard strange noises. Steps, he thought, something following him from the house. He spun around to see, and at that moment some flying thing hit him in the face. Devin screamed and ran into the stable. Almost immediately he realized that the wind had gusted just then and broken a branch from the tree. It had hit him.

But at least he was in the stable now. And then lightning struck again, lightning so brilliant that even Branwen's brown coat looked stark white. Everything in the stable was stark except for a shadow that flickered at Branwen's feet in front of the manager. A black thing. And yellow eyes gleaming from the blackness.

There was pitch-darkness again, and Devin groped his way along Branwen to kneel by her feet. Thunder rolled and rolled like shots fired from a cannon. Devin bent to Sdhoirm, who whimpered his greeting.

In the darkness Devin felt the soft tongue lick his hand. From behind, Branwen nudged Devin. She didn't lick, but just mooed in a soft, concerned way, and stuck her head close to Sdhoirm.

Devin put his hand under the wolf's head. He couldn't see what was wrong, he could only feel the weak, limp body of the wolf. The shoulder joint that Devin remembered as being hard and lean now felt loose, as though bone and flesh had separated. Sdhoirm whimpered from pain. The wolf's fur was wet, and Devin thought that it was from the rain; but when the stable lit again, Devin saw the wetness was blood.

It wasn't just the wolf's front shoulder that was hurt, but his back leg as well, twisted in some unnatural way. The wolf's entire body was like a gaping wound. There didn't seem to be any part of him that had not been torn, ripped, or crushed in some way. One of Sdhoirm's ears was completely ripped off, and a chunk was gone from the black tip of his nose. Blood seeped slowly but continuously from the broken body. Devin gently lifted the twisted leg and tried to straighten it. The wolf whined.

The stable lit once more, and for the first time Devin noticed that his lucky rabbit's foot was still hanging around Sdhoirm's neck where he had hung it three years ago. The rabbit's foot was blood-soaked too. Sdhoirm stretched his neck so that he could touch Devin's hand. He licked it weakly and whined.

Devin knew that the wolf was dying, that there was nothing that could be done to save him. All he could do now was to sit with him and touch him gently with his hands to try and ease the suffering. Devin touched the lump in the wolf's shoulder where the first shot had lodged and the flesh had regrown around it.

For years Sdhoirm had been running in the wild, always pursued. Once he had been poisoned. Terrible convulsions had burned his belly, as though there was a fire in his guts for days. He had grown weak with vomiting, but he had recovered and had grown cunning.

Sometimes, as he wandered through the hills, the wolf had heard the boy's voice, and many times he had tried to come close to him, but always the baying of hounds and the guns of men came between them.

Tonight there had been more hounds and more guns, and tonight the wolf had been trapped by a pack of hounds on the edge of a sharp cliff, and he had fought. The hounds had ripped away chunks of his flesh and crushed the bones in his hip. He had managed to kill two of the hounds. And then there was a shot. A burning sensation lodged like a stake in the wolf's throat, so that every breath burned as though he were inhaling fire.

The burning metal sent him reeling on his hind legs, and he tumbled into the river below. The water carried him crashing like a stick against the rocks and rapids, but the river quieted in a bend and he crawled out, dragging his crippled leg behind. The dogs had left him for dead, which was just as well, for now he was dying, but before he died, he wanted to return to the place that had once been home.

Dragging his shattered leg behind him, he crawled through the forest and into the town and found his way to the stable, collapsing at the cow's front feet. And she, knowing that something was dreadfully wrong, had lifted her voice and bawled until Devin had come out. And now that Devin was here with him, the wolf was ready to die, and he let his head slip away softly from the boy's hand.

Pain traveled through the wolf's body, but the boy was touching him now, and the boy's hands felt so gentle.

Devin took the leg that had been mangled by the hound pack and lifted it. The pain shot through

Sdhoirm and he yelped, but Devin turned the leg so that it was in its proper place and Sdhoirm lay quiet once more.

Devin could feel life seeping from the wolf. He tried to put his hands over the wounds to stop the blood, but it was too late. He lifted hay and gently put it over Sdhoirm to keep him warm. He tried not to cry. Sdhoirm was going to a safe place, a faraway place, someplace warm and soft. The wolf's mother would be there, waiting for him, and other wolves.

At nights in the forest, Devin had heard Sdhoirm lift his voice in a call to others, and not one wolf had answered him, for in all the hills and forests of Ireland and in all the plains, there was not another wolf left. Now, for the first time, Sdhoirm would see other wolves, hundreds of wolves, and he would be able to lift his voice and howl with them.

A new flash of lightning speared the blackness, making the yellow eyes burn bright. Sdhoirm let out a single long, lonely howl, and then his head dropped and he was still.

Devin began to cry. "Sdhoirm! Sdhoirm! Wake up! Please, wake up. Please, God! Don't let him die." And his tears fell on Sdhoirm's bloody fur.

Branwen touched the wolf with her nose, and then she touched Devin's shoulder, and she too stood still.

Lightning struck with repeated brilliance, forking through the blackness. The earth beneath Devin's feet shook with the fury of the storm, and the wind began to howl like a wild thing. Devin saw that the wolf's yellow eyes were closed, and in the wind he seemed to hear the terrible howl of all the wolves that had been killed in Ireland. Their cries seemed to rise with the wind, and the rain began to fall, and it seemed to Devin that Nature was weeping — for the last wolf of Ireland was dead.

Elona Malterre describes *The Last Wolf of Ireland* as a dramatization of "issues concerning love, the futility of violence, and the recognition that human beings must respect all living things."

Born in France and raised in Calgary, Alberta, Canada, where she now lives, Elona Malterre is a recipient of the Bliss Carman Award for poetry. Her love of Ireland was sparked when she took a course in Irish literature leading to an M.A. in English. She has taught literature and creative writing at the University of Calgary and at Mount Royal College, where she currently teaches part-time.

Elona Malterre is the author of two historical novels for adults, *The Celts* and *Mistress of the Eagles*. *The Last Wolf of Ireland* was written at the request of her daughter, Alexandra.